The Circus Boys on the Plains

Edgar B. P. Darlington

Contents

CHAPTER I ON THE OWNER'S PRIVATE CAR 7

CHAPTER II OFF FOR NEW FIELDS 17

CHAPTER III COMING TO AN UNDERSTANDING 23

CHAPTER IV INTRODUCED TO THE CREW 27

CHAPTER V THE MIDNIGHT ALARM 34

CHAPTER VI ALMOST A TRAGEDY 39

CHAPTER VII THE FIRST DAY'S EXPERIENCE 44

CHAPTER VIII THE CIRCUS BOY WINS 50

CHAPTER IX TEDDY GETS INTO TROUBLE 57

CHAPTER X A SURPRISE, INDEED 63

CHAPTER XI THREE CHEERS AND A TIGER 71

CHAPTER XII FACING AN EMERGENCY 77

CHAPTER XIII A BAFFLED CAR MANAGER 84

CHAPTER XIV TEDDY WRITES A LETTER 91

CHAPTER XV IN AN EXCITING RACE 96

CHAPTER XVI A BATTLE OF WITS 102

CHAPTER XVII THE CHARGE OF THE PASTE BRIGADE............................107

CHAPTER XVIII THE MISSING SHOW CARS 112

CHAPTER XIX PHIL'S DARING PLAN 118

CHAPTER XX ON A WILDCAT RUN 127

CHAPTER XXI IN A PERILOUS POSITION 133

CHAPTER XXII A DASH FOR LIBERTY 138

CHAPTER XXIII THE DESERTED VILLAGE..142

CHAPTER XXIV CONCLUSION 149

THE CIRCUS BOYS ON THE PLAINS

BY

Edgar B. P. Darlington

CHAPTER I
ON THE OWNER'S PRIVATE CAR

Bates!"

The voice of James Sparling rose above even the roar of the storm.

A uniformed attendant stepped into the little office tent occupied by the owner of the Great Sparling Combined Shows. Shaking the water from his dripping cap, he brought a hand to his forehead in precise military salute.

"How's the storm coming, Bates?" demanded the showman, with an amused twinkle in his eyes as he noted the bedraggled condition of his messenger.

"She's coming wet, sir," was the comprehensive reply.

And indeed "she" was. The gale was roaring over the circus lot, momentarily threatening to wrench the billowing circus tents from their fastenings, lift them high in the air preparatory to distributing them over the surrounding country. Guy ropes were straining at their anchorages, center and quarter poles were beating a nervous tattoo on the sodden turf. The rain was driving over the circus lot in blinding sheets.

The night was not ideal for a circus performance. However, the showmen uttered no protest, going about their business as methodically as if the air were warm and balmy, the moon and stars shining down over the scene complacently.

Now and again, as the wind shifted for a moment toward the showman's swaying office tent, the blare of the band off under the big top told him the show was moving merrily on.

"Bates, you are almost human at times. I had already observed that the storm was coming wet," replied the showman.

"Yes, sir."

"I have reason to be aware of the fact that 'she is coming wet,' as you so admirably put it. My feet are at this moment in a puddle of water that is now three inches above my ankles. Why shouldn't I know?"

"Yes, sir," agreed the patient attendant.

"What I want to know is how are the tents standing the blow?"

"Very well, sir."

"As long as there is a stitch of canvas over your head you take it for granted that the tops are all right, eh?"

"Yes, sir."

"The emergency gang is on duty, of course?"

"They're out in the wet, sir."

"Of course; that is where they belong on a night like this. But what were you doing out there? You have no business that calls you outside."

"I was helping a lady, sir."

"Helping a lady?"

"Yes, sir."

"What lady?"

"The English Fat Girl got mired on the lot, sir, and I was helping to get her out," answered the attendant solemnly.

"Pshaw!"

"Yes, sir."

"You will please attend to your own business after this. If the English Fat Girl gets mired again we will have the elephant trainer bring over one of the bulls and haul her out. She won't be so anxious to get stalled after that, I'm thinking," snapped the showman.

"Yes, sir."

"What act is on now under the big top?"

"The ground tumblers are in the ring, sir."

Mr. Sparling reflected briefly.

"Has Mr. Forrest finished his work for the evening?"

"I think so, sir. He should be off by this time."

"Can you get to the dressing tent without finishing the job of drowning at which you already have made such a good start?" demanded the showman quizzically.

"Yes, sir," grinned Bates.

"Then, go there."

The attendant started to leave the tent.

"Come back here!" bellowed the showman.

Bates turned patiently. He was not unused to the strange whims of his employer.

"What are you going to do when you get to the dressing tent?"

"I don't know, sir."

"I thought not. You are an intelligent animal, Bates. Now listen!"

"Yes, sir."

Mr. Sparling scowled, surveying his messenger with narrowed eyes.

"Tell Mr. Philip Forrest that I wish to see him in my private car at the 'runs,'"--meaning that part of the railroad yards where the show had unloaded early that morning.

"Yes, sir."

"Wait! You seem anxious to get wet! Have the men strike my tent at once. It is likely to strike itself if they do not get busy pretty quick," added the showman, rising.

The messenger saluted, then hurried out into the driving storm, while Mr. Sparling methodically gathered up the papers he had been studying, stuffing them in an inside coat pocket.

"A fine, mellow night," he said to himself, peering out through the flap as he drew on his oilskins. Pulling the brim of his sombrero down over his eyes he stalked out into the storm.

A quick glance up into the skies told his experienced eyes that the worst of the storm had passed, and that there was now little danger of a blow-down that night. He started off across the circus lot, splashing through the mud and water, bound for his comfortable private car that lay on a siding about half a mile from the circus grounds.

He found a scene of bustle and excitement in the railroad yards, where a small army of men were rushing the work of loading the menagerie wagons on the first section, for the train was going out in three sections that night.

"It is a peculiar fact," muttered the showman, "that the worse the weather is, the louder the men seem called upon to yell. However, if yelling makes them feel any the less wet, I don't know why I should object."

The showman quickly changed his wet clothes and settled himself at the desk in his cosy office on board the private car. He had been there something like half an hour when the buzzing of an electric bell called the porter to the door of the car.

A moment later and Phil Forrest appeared at the door of the car.

"You sent for me, did you not, Mr. Sparling?"

"Why, good evening, Phil," greeted the showman, looking up quickly with a welcoming smile on his face.

"I call it a very bad evening, sir."

"Very well, we will revise our statement. Bad evening, Phil!"

"Same to you, Mr. Sparling," laughed the lad. "Yes, I think that fits the case very well indeed."

"And now that we have observed the formalities, come in and sit down. Are you wet?"

"No; I went to my car and changed before coming in. I thought a few minutes' delay would make no difference. Had you sent for me on the lot I would have reported more promptly."

"Quite right, my boy. No, there was nothing urgent. The storm did not interfere much with the performance, did it?"

"No. The audience was a little nervous at one time, but the scare quickly passed off."

"Where's your friend?"

"Teddy Tucker?"

"Yes."

"He was having an argument with the Strongest Man on Earth when I left the dressing tent," laughed Phil. "It was becoming quite heated."

"Over what?"

"Oh, Teddy insisted on sitting on the strong man's trunk while he took off his tights. There was a mud hole in front of Teddy's trunk and he did not wish to get his feet wet and muddy."

"So the Strongest Man on Earth had to wait, eh?" questioned the showman with an amused smile.

"Yes. Teddy was threatening to thrash him if he did not keep off until he got his shoes on."

Mr. Sparling leaned back, laughing heartily.

"Your friend Teddy is getting to be a very belligerent young man, I fear."

"*Getting* to be?"

"Yes."

"It is my opinion that he always has been. Teddy can stir up more trouble, and with less provocation, than anyone I ever knew. But, you had something you wished to say to me, did you not?"

"To be sure I had. Something quite important. Have you had your lunch?"

"No; I came directly to the train from the lot."

"I am glad of that. I thought you would, so I ordered supper for two spread in the dining compartment. It must be ready by this time. Come. We will talk and eat at the same time. We have no need to hurry."

The showman and the Circus Boy made their way to the dining compartment, where a small table had been spread for them, which, with its pretty china, cut glass and brightly polished silver, made a very attractive appearance.

"This looks good to me," smiled Phil appreciatively.

"Especially on a night like this," answered Mr. Sparling. "Be seated, and we will talk while we are waiting for supper to be served."

Readers of the preceding volumes of this series will need no introduction to Phil Forrest and Teddy Tucker. They well remember how the Circus Boys so unexpectedly made their entry into the sawdust arena in "THE CIRCUS BOYS ON THE FLYING RINGS" after Phil by his quick wit had prevented a serious accident to the lion cage and perhaps the escape of the dangerous beast itself. Both boys had quickly worked their way into the arena, and after many thrilling experiences became full-fledged circus performers.

Again in "THE CIRCUS BOYS ACROSS THE CONTINENT," the lads won new laurels on the tanbark. It will be recalled, too, how Phil Forrest at the imminent risk of his own life trailed down and captured a desperate man, one of the circus employees who, having been discharged, had followed the Sparling Show, seeking to revenge himself upon it. It will be remembered that in order to capture the fellow, the Circus Boy was obliged to leap from a rapidly moving train and plunge down a high embankment.

But their exciting experiences were by no means at an end. The life of the showman is full of excitement and it seemed as if Teddy and Phil Forrest met with more than their share in "THE CIRCUS BOYS IN DIXIE LAND." Phil Forrest, while performing a mission for his employer, was caught by a rival circus owner, held captive for some days, then forced to perform in the rival's circus ring, leaping through rings of fire in a bareback riding act. The details of Phil's exciting escape from his captors are well remembered, as will be his long, weary journey over the railroad ties in his ring costume. It was in this story that the battle of the elephants was described, all due to the shrewd planning of Phil Forrest.

The following season found the Great Sparling Shows following a new route. In "THE CIRCUS BOYS ON THE MISSISSIPPI," the lads embarked with the circus, on boats, which carried them from town to town along the big river. It was on this trip that Phil Forrest met with the most thrilling experience of his life, and it was only his own pluck and endurance that saved him from a watery grave at the bottom of the Mississippi.

And now, for the fifth season, the Circus Boys are found under canvas again, headed for the far west.

"How are things going with you?" questioned Mr. Sparling after the two had seated themselves at the table in the dining compartment.

"Rather slowly, Mr. Sparling."

"How is that?"

"I haven't enough to do this season. I am afraid I shall get lazy, unless you give me something else to do."

"Let me see; how many acts have you this season?"

"I am on the flying trapeze, then I do a single bareback riding act and a double with Little Dimples, the same as I did last season."

The showman nodded reflectively.

"Besides which, you attend to numerous business details for me, manage the side shows, keep an eye on the candy butchers, make yourself responsible for the menagerie tent and other things too numerous to mention. Yes; you should have a few more things to do," grinned the showman. "I could run this show with a dozen men like you, Phil. In all my circus experience I never saw your equal."

Phil flushed. He did not like to be complimented. He did his work because he loved it, not wholly for the handsome salary that he was now drawing from the little red ticket wagon every week. Phil was ambitious; he hoped, as has been said before, to have a show of his own someday, and he let no day pass that he did not add to his store of knowledge regarding the circus business.

In this ambition Mr. Sparling encouraged him, in fact did everything possible to aid the lad in acquiring a far-reaching knowledge of the vocation he had chosen for his lifework.

"Thank you, Mr. Sparling. Let's talk about something else."

"We will eat first. You probably will enjoy that more than you do my compliments."

"I am sure of it," answered the lad with a twinkle in his eyes.

"I have been thinking of giving you some additional work."

Phil glanced up at his employer with quickened interest.

"Yes, I am thinking of closing you."

"You mean you are thinking of dropping me from the show?" asked the lad, gazing at the showman with steady, inquiring eyes.

"Well, I should hardly say that. I am afraid the Sparling Show could not get along without you. I am thinking very seriously of transferring you."

"Transferring me?" wondered Phil.

"Yes. By the way, do you know much about the advance work, the work ahead of the show?"

"Very little. I might say nothing at all, except what I have picked up by reading the reports of the car managers, together with the letters you write to these men."

"That is all right, as far as it goes, but there is a deal more to the advertising department of a show than you will ever learn from reports and correspondence."

"So I should imagine."

"Yes; the success, the very existence of a circus is dependent upon the work of the men ahead of it. Let that work be neglected and you would see how soon business would drop off and the gate receipts dwindle, until, one day, the show would find itself stranded."

"Nothing could strand the Sparling Show," interposed Phil.

"You are mistaken. Bad management would put this show out of business in two months' time. That is a point that I cannot impress upon you too strongly. Any business will fail if not properly attended to, but a circus is the most hazardous of them all."

"But the risk is worth taking," remarked Phil.

"It is. For instance, when a show has a business of sixteen or eighteen thousand dollars a day for several weeks, it rather repays one for all the trouble and worry he has gone through."

"I should say it does," answered Phil, his eyes lighting up appreciatively.

"And now we come to the point I have been getting at."

"Yes; what is it you have in mind for me?"

"I am going to ask you to join the advance for the rest of the season, Phil."

"I, join the advance?" questioned the lad in a surprised tone.

"Yes."

"And leave the show?"

"That will be a necessity, much as I regret to have you do so."

Phil's face took on a solemn expression.

"How would you like that?"

"I do not know, Mr. Sparling. I am afraid I should not know what to do with myself away from the glitter and the excitement of the big show."

"Excitement? My dear boy, you will find all the excitement you want ahead of the show. As for work, the work ahead is never finished. There is always plenty to do after you have finished your day's work. Besides, this branch of the business you must familiarize yourself with, if you are to go later into the executive branch of the circus business."

"I am ready to go wherever you may wish to send me, Mr. Sparling," said the young man in a quiet tone.

"I knew you would be," smiled the showman.

"Where will you send me, and what am I to do?" asked Phil, now growing interested in the prospect of the change.

"I have decided to send you out on Advertising Car Number Three. That is the busiest car of the three in advance of the show. You ask what you are to do. I will answer--***everything!***"

"Car Three," mused the Circus Boy.

"Yes; it is in charge of Mr. Snowden," continued the showman with a twinkle in his eyes, but which Phil in his preoccupation failed to observe. "I am thinking that Snowden will give you all you want to do, and perhaps a little more."

"When do you wish me to join?"

"At once."

"Now?"

"You may start as soon as you are ready."

"I am ready, now," replied the lad promptly.

"I did not mean for you to leave in quite such a hurry as that," laughed Mr. Sparling. "Besides, this is rather a bad night to make a change. Take your time, get your things in shape, and leave when you get ready."

"Does Mr. Snowden know I am to join him?"

"Yes; I have already written him to that effect--that is, I told him you probably would join at an early day."

"Where is Car Three now?"

Mr. Sparling consulted his route card.

"It is in Madison, Wisconsin, today. This car keeps about four weeks ahead of the show, you know. We are in Flint, Michigan, today. Do you think you can get away tomorrow?"

"Certainly. Where do we show tomorrow?"

"Saginaw."

"It will be an easy jump from there to Madison."

"Yes; but you will not catch the car at Madison. I think you had better plan to join them at St. Paul the day after tomorrow. Will that suit you?"

"Yes. I suppose my dressing-room trunk will be carried right along with the show?"

"Of course. You will close your season before the show itself does; then you can return to us, though I shall not expect you to perform. You no doubt will be a little rusty by that time."

"I should say I would be. But, Mr. Sparling--" added the boy, a sudden thought coming to him.

"Yes?"

"What about Teddy? Does he remain with the show?"

"Teddy? I had forgotten all about that little rascal. Yes, he-- but wait a moment. Upon reflection I think perhaps he had better go along with you. He wants to own a show one of these days, doesn't he?"

"I believe he does," smiled Phil.

"Then this will be a good experience for him. Besides, I should be afraid to trust him around this outfit if you were not here to look after him. He would put the whole show out of business first thing I knew. Yes, he had better go with you. And another thing--salaries in the advance are not the same, you know."

"I am aware of the fact, sir."

"You will draw the same salaries that other employees of Number Three do, and in addition to this I shall send you both my personal checks, so that you will be drawing the same money you now are."

"It is not necessary," protested Phil.

Mr. Sparling waved the objection aside.

"It is my plan. Go to your car and tell your friend to get ready now, and report to me in the morning at Saginaw for further instructions."

Phil rose. His face was flushed. He was now full of anticipation for the new life before him. And it was to be a new life indeed--a life full of astonishing experiences and adventures.

Phil bade his employer good night, and hurried away to his own car to tell the news to Teddy.

CHAPTER II
OFF FOR NEW FIELDS

Teddy, Teddy, wake up!" commanded Phil, hauling his companion from his berth in the sleeping car.

Teddy scrambled out into the aisle of the car and promptly showed fight.

"Here, what are you doing, waking me up this time of the night?" he demanded.

"I have great news."

"News?" questioned the boy, showing some slight signs of interest in the announcement.

"Yes, news, and good news, too."

"All right, I'm easy. What is it?"

"We are to join the advance."

"Advance of what?"

"The advance of the Sparling Shows, of course," glowed Phil.

Teddy grew thoughtful.

"What, and leave the show?"

"Certainly."

"Not for mine!"

"Oh, yes, you will! You know, we wish to learn all we can, and neither of us knows anything about that end of the business. It is a splendid opportunity, and we should be very grateful to Mr. Sparling for giving us the chance. Besides, it will be a very pleasant life. We shall be traveling in a private car, with no responsibilities beyond our work. Will it not be fine?"

"I--I don't know. I shall have to try it first. I decline to commit myself in advance. When do we go?"

"Tomorrow."

"Pshaw! Boss Sparling seems to be in an awful hurry to get rid of us. All right, I'll go. I need a rest, anyway--for my health. I've been working too hard so far this season."

"Too bad about you," scoffed Phil. "We leave from Saginaw as early tomorrow as we can get away. We shall have to get a few things from our dressing-tent trunks, then pack up the things we do not need, sending them on with the show."

"Do I take my donkey?" questioned Teddy, half humorously.

"Your mule? The idea! Now, what would you do with a donkey on an advance car, I should like to know?"

"He might make things interesting for the rest of the crowd."

"I should say he would! But, from what little I know of the advance, you will have plenty to interest you without having an ill-tempered donkey along. Good night, Teddy. This is our last night with the show for a long time to come."

Phil made his way to his own berth, where he promptly went to sleep, putting from his mind until the morrow all thought of what lay before him.

Early the next morning both lads were awake; by the time their section pulled in at Saginaw they had nearly completed the packing of their personal baggage.

The rest was quickly accomplished, after they had eaten their breakfast under the cook tent. All preparations made, a final interview with Mr. Sparling had, and good-byes said, the Circus Boys boarded a train just as the strains of the circus band were borne to their ears.

"The parade is on," said Phil as their train moved out.

"And we are not there to ride in it. We'll have to get up some sort of a parade for Car Number Three, I'm thinking," smiled Teddy.

Late that afternoon the boys reached St. Paul. After considerable searching about they finally found Car Number Three. Mr. Snowden was not on board, so, telling the porter who they were, the lads made themselves comfortable in the office of the car, a roomy compartment, nicely furnished, equipped with two folding berths, a desk, easy chairs and other conveniences.

"This is pretty soft, I'm thinking," decided Teddy.

"It is very nice, if that is what you mean," corrected Phil.

"That's what I mean. Do we live in here?"

"No; I should imagine we are to berth at the other end of the car."

"Let's go look at it."

The other end of the car comprised one long apartment with folding berths and benches for laying out the lithographs. At the far end was a steam boiler, used in making paste with which to post the bills. That compartment had nothing either of elegance or comfort.

"Do the men sleep on those shelves up there?" questioned Teddy of the porter.

"Shelves, sir? Hi calls them berths, sir," answered the porter, who was an Englishman.

"Humph!"

"What do you think of our new home, Teddy?" smiled Phil.

"I've seen better," grumbled the Circus Boy. "I think I prefer the stateroom. Where's the boss?"

"He's out just now looking over the work."

Teddy, with a scowl on his face, went outside to take a look at the car from the outside. The car was a bright red, with the name of the Sparling Shows spread over its sides in gilded letters.

"If the inside were half as good-looking as the outside, it would be some car," was Teddy's conclusion, after walking all around the car. "I think I'll go back and join the show."

"Oh, be sensible, Teddy," chided Phil. "We shall be very comfortable after we once get settled. Here comes Mr. Snowden, I think."

Approaching them, the boys saw a thin, nervous-appearing man of perhaps forty-five years of age.

"Are you Mr. Snowden?" asked Phil, politely.

"Yes; what do you want?"

"I am Phil Forrest, and this is my friend, Teddy Tucker. We have come on to join the car."

Mr. Snowden looked the lads over critically.

"Humph!" he said. "Come inside."

Whether or not his survey of them had been satisfactory neither lad knew.

"Now, what are you going to do on this car?" demanded the car manager sharply, when they had seated themselves in his office.

"That is for you to say, sir. We are at your disposal," replied Phil.

"What can you do?"

"We do not know. This is entirely new work for us. We have been performers back with the show, you know."

"Humph! Nice bunch to ring in on an advertising car!" grunted the manager. "Either of you know how to put up paper?"

"I think not."

"What do you mean by paper?" interposed Teddy.

The manager groaned.

"You don't know what paper is?"

"No, sir."

"Paper is advertising matter, any kind of show bills that are posted on bill-boards, barns or any other old place where we get the chance. Everything is paper on an advertising car. Forrest, I think I'll send you out on a country route tomorrow. Know what a country route is?"

"I think so."

"Well, in case you do not, I will tell you. Every day we send out men to post bills through the country. The routes are laid out by the contracting agent long before we get to a town. You go out in a livery rig, and you will have to drive from thirty to forty miles a day. You are an aerial performer, are you not?"

"Yes, sir."

"Then you will be able to climb barns all right. We will call you Car Number Three's barn-climber. We'll see how good a performer you really are. For the first few days I will send you out with one of the billposters; after that you will have to go it alone. If you are no good, back you go. Understand?"

"I think so. I shall do the best I can."

"And what do I do?" demanded Teddy.

The car manager eyed him disapprovingly.

"What do you do?"

"Yes."

"I have a nice gentlemanly job laid out for you. You will operate the steam boiler and make up the paste for the next day. You'll wish you had stayed back with the show before I get through with you."

"And I'll go there, too, if you talk like that to me," retorted Teddy, flushing angrily.

"What's that? What's that?" snapped the manager. "See here, young man, I am in charge of this car. You will do as I tell you, and if you get noisy about it I'll show you how we do things on an advertising car. Get out of here before I throw you out."

"See here, you, I won't be talked to like that. I'll wring your neck for you, some fine day, first thing you know!" bellowed Teddy, now thoroughly aroused.

The manager grabbed the lad by the shoulders and shot him through the screen doors before Teddy had an opportunity to object.

Teddy, red-faced and boiling with rage, was about to project himself into the stateroom again when Phil motioned him to go away. Teddy did so reluctantly.

"Where do we sleep, Mr. Snowden?" inquired Phil, hoping to get the car manager in a more gentle frame of mind by changing the subject.

"Sleep on the roof, sleep in the cellar! I don't care where you sleep! You get out of here, too, unless you want me to throw you out!"

"I think you had better not do that, sir." Phil's voice was cool and pleasant.

"What's that! What's that! You dare to talk back to me. I'll--"

"Wait a moment, Mr. Snowden. We might as well understand each other at the beginning."

The car manager's words seemed to stick in his throat. He gazed at the slender young fellow before him in amazement. Mr. Snowden was unused to having a man in his employ talk back to him, and for the moment it looked as though trouble were brewing in the stateroom of Car Number Three.

"Say it!" he exploded.

"I have very little to say, sir. But what I have to say will be to the point. I am well aware that discipline must be preserved here as well as back with the show. I shall always look up to you as my superior, and treat you in a gentlemanly and respectful manner. I shall hope that you, also, will treat me in a gentlemanly manner as long as I deserve it, at least."

"You--you threaten me, you young cub--you--"

"No; I do not threaten you. I am simply seeking to come to a friendly understanding with you."

"And--and if--if I decide to treat you as I do the rest of my men--what then?" sneered the manager.

"That depends. I can answer that question when I see how you do treat them. From what I have seen, I should imagine they do not lead a very happy existence," continued the Circus Boy with a pleasant smile.

"If I keep you on this car I'll use you as I please, and the quicker you understand that the better. Now, what do you propose to do?"

"I propose," said Phil, still preserving an even tone, "to do my duty and at the same time keep my self-respect. I propose, if you persist in directing insulting language at me, to give you a thrashing that will last you all the rest of the season."

Teddy, who had sat down on a pile of railroad ties beside the tracks, could see and hear all that was going on in the stateroom.

"Soak him, Phil!" howled the boy on the tie pile.

Snowden's eyes blazed and his fingers opened and closed convulsively.

With an angry growl he hurled himself straight at Phil Forrest.

CHAPTER III
COMING TO AN UNDERSTANDING

B e careful, Mr. Snowden!" warned the Circus Boy, stepping out of harm's way. "I am not looking for trouble, but I shall defend myself."

"I'll teach you to talk back to me. I'll--"

Just then the car manager stumbled over a chair and went down with a crash, smashing the chair to splinters.

"Mr. Sparling will not tolerate anything of this sort, I am sure," added Phil.

By this time, the manager was once more on his feet. His rage was past all control. With a roar of rage Snowden grabbed up a rung of the broken chair and charged his slender young antagonist.

A faint flush leaped into the face of Phil Forrest. His eyes narrowed a little, but in no other way did he show that his temper was in the least ruffled.

The chair rung was brought down with a vicious sweep, but to Snowden's surprise the weapon failed to reach the head of the smiling Circus Boy.

Then Phil got into action.

Like a flash he leaped forward, and the car manager found his wrists clasped in a vise-like grip.

"Let go of me!" he roared, struggling with all his might to free himself, failing in which he began to kick.

Phil gave the wrists a skillful twist, which brought another howl from Snowden, this time a howl of pain.

"I am not looking for trouble, sir. Will you listen to reason?" urged the lad.

"I'll--I'll--"

Snowden did not finish what he had started to say. Instead he moaned with pain, writhing helplessly in the iron grip of Phil Forrest.

"Do you give up? Have you had enough?"

"*No!*" gritted the car manager.

The Circus Boy tightened his grip ever so little.

"How about it?"

"Give him an extra twist for me," shouted Teddy.

"I give in! Let go quick! You'll break my wrists!"

"You promise to carry this thing no further if I release you?"

"I said I have had enough," cried Snowden angrily.

"That won't do. Will you agree to let me alone, if I release you now?" persisted Phil.

"Yes, yes! I've had all I want. This joke has gone far enough."

"Joke?"

"Yes."

"You have a queer idea of jokes," smiled Phil, releasing his man and stepping back, but keeping a wary eye on the car manager, as the latter settled back into a chair, rubbing his wrists. They still pained him severely.

"I am sorry if I hurt you, Mr. Snowden. But I had to defend myself in some way. I could have been much more violent, but I did not wish to be unnecessarily so."

"You were rough enough. I've got no use for a fellow who can't take a joke without getting all riled up over it. Get out of here!"

"What are you doing at this end of the car?" snarled the manager to Henry, the English porter, who had been peering into the office, wide-eyed. He had been a witness to the disturbance, but at the manager's command he hastily withdrew to his own end of the car.

"Shall we shake hands and be friends now, Mr. Snowden?" asked Phil.

"Shake hands?"

"Yes, of course."

"No. I'll not shake hands with you. I want nothing further to do with you. Either you get off this car, or I do. We can't both live on it at the same time."

"So far as I am concerned, we can do so easily," answered the Circus Boy.

"I said either you or I would have to get off, and I mean exactly what I said."

The manager wheeled his chair about, facing his desk, and wrote the following telegram:

Mr. James Sparling,

Saginaw, Michigan.

I demand that you call back the two boys who joined my car today. Either they close or I do. They're a couple of young ruffians. If they remain another day I'll not be responsible for what I do to them.

Snowden.

The car manager handed the message to Phil. "Read it," he snapped.

Phil glanced through the message, smiling broadly as he returned it to the manager.

"That certainly is plain and to the point."

"I'm glad you think so. Take that message to the telegraph office, and send it at once."

"Yes, sir."

Mr. Snowden had expected a refusal, but Phil rose obediently and left the car. He took the message to a telegraph office, Teddy accompanying him.

"Why didn't you finish him while you were about it, Phil?" demanded Teddy. "You had him just to rights."

"I did quite enough as it was, Teddy. I am very sorry for what I did, but it had to come."

"It did. If you hadn't done it I should have had to," nodded Teddy rather pompously. "But I shouldn't have let him off as easily as you did. I certainly would have given him a rough-and-tumble."

"It is a bad enough beginning as it is. Now, Teddy, I want you to behave yourself and not stir up any trouble--"

"Stir up trouble? Well, I like that. Who's been stirring up trouble around here, I'd like to know. Answer me that!"

"I accept the rebuke," laughed Phil. "I am the guilty one this time, and I'm heartily ashamed to admit it at that."

"What do you think Mr. Sparling will do?"

"I don't know. I can't help but think he had some purpose in sending us on to join this car, other than that which he told us. However, time will tell. We are in for an unpleasant season, but we must make the best of our opportunity and learn all we can about this end of the business."

"I've learned enough this afternoon to last me for a whole season," answered Teddy grimly.

By the time they returned to the car the men had come in from the country routes, as had the lithographers who had been placing bills in store windows about the town.

"He's at it again," grinned Teddy, as the voice of the manager was heard roaring at the men. Snowden was charging up and down the car venting his wrath on the men, threatening, browbeating, expressing his opinion of all billposters in language more picturesque than elegant. Not a man replied to his tirade.

"Evidently they are used to that sort of treatment," nodded Phil. "Well it doesn't go with me at all. Come on; let's go in and see what it's all about."

CHAPTER IV
INTRODUCED TO THE CREW

A nd the next man who puts up only two hundred sheets in a day gets off this car!" concluded Snowden with a wave of the hand that took in every man in the car. "Get in your reports, and get them in quick, or I'll fire the whole bunch of you now!" he roared, turning and striding to his office, where he jerked the sliding door shut with a bang that shook the car.

"Well, the boss has 'em bad tonight, for sure," exclaimed Billy Conley who bore the title of assistant car manager, but who was no more manager than was Henry, the English porter.

"Hello, who are you?" demanded one of the men, as Phil and Teddy stepped in through the rear door of the coach.

"Good evening, boys," greeted Phil easily.

All eyes were turned on the newcomers.

"Howdy, fellows," said Teddy good-naturedly. "Fine, large evening."

Everybody laughed.

"Are you the boys who joined out today, from back with the show?" asked Conley.

"Yes. Let me introduce myself. I am Phil Forrest and this, my companion, is Teddy Tucker. We're green as grass, and we shall have to impose upon your good nature to set us straight."

The Circus Boys had won the good opinion of the men of Car Three at the outset.

"That's the talk," agreed Billy. "Line up here and I'll introduce you to the bunch. The skinny fellow over there by the boiler is Chief Rain-in-the-Face. The one next to him is Slivers. The freakish looking gentleman standing at my right is

Krao, the Missing Link. On my left is Baby Egawa--"

"Otherwise known as Rosie the Pig," added a voice.

"Everybody on an advance car has a nickname, you know. You'll forget your real names, if you stay on an advance car long enough. I couldn't remember mine if I didn't get a letter occasionally to remind me of it, and sometimes I almost feel as if I was opening another fellow's letters when I open my own."

"Glad to know you, boys," smiled Phil. "Do you know where we are to sleep?"

"See that pile of paper up there?"

"Yes."

"Well, it's that or the floor for yours. All the rest of the berths are occupied, unless the Boss is going to let you sleep in the office with him."

"I rather think he will not invite us. He seems to be in a huff about something tonight," answered Phil dryly, at which there was a loud laugh.

"What's this Johnnie Bull tells me about a roughhouse in the office this afternoon?" demanded Conley suddenly.

"I would rather not talk about that," replied Phil, coloring.

"Come here, you Englishman, and tell us all about it. Our friend is too modest."

The porter did not respond quickly enough to suit the men so they pounced upon him and tossed him to the top of a pile of paper.

"Now, talk up, or its the paste can for yours," they demanded.

Henry rather haltingly described what he had seen in the stateroom that afternoon, describing in detail how Phil had worsted the manager of the car.

When the recital had been concluded, all hands turned and surveyed Phil curiously.

"Well, who would have thought it?" wondered Rosie, in an awed voice.

Krao, the Missing Link, and Baby Egawa sidled up to Phil and gingerly felt his arm muscles.

"Woof!" exclaimed the Baby. "Bad medicine! Heap big muscle!"

"That's so. I had forgotten you boys were performers back with the show," nodded Billy. "What are you up here for--learning this end of the business?"

"Yes; that is what we are here for," answered Phil. "Mr. Sparling wished us to do so."

"You have come to a good place to learn it," emphasized Conley. "But you'll have to fight your way through. You have done a mighty good job in downing the Boss, but look out for him. He'll never forget it. If he doesn't get you fired, he will get even with you in some other way."

Phil laughed.

"I'll do my duty. But I am not afraid of him. Are all car managers like Mr. Snowden?"

"Most of them. Some better, some worse. They think they are not doing their duty, earning their meal-tickets, unless they are Roaring Jakes. But Snowden is the worst ever. He has the meanest disposition of any man I ever knew. This is his first season on Number Three, and I shouldn't be surprised if it were his last. I hear Boss Sparling doesn't take to him. Know anything about that?"

Phil shook his head.

"Why do you let him treat you as he does?"

"Let him? Well, I'll tell you confidentially. Most of us have families to support. Some of us have wives; others mothers and sisters to look after. It's put up with the roast or get out. And let me tell you, the Boss isn't slow about closing out a fellow he doesn't like. He'll fire you at the drop of the hat."

"I'm hungry; where do we eat?" interrupted Teddy.

"Eat?"

"Sure! Don't you fellows in advance eat?"

"Well, we go through the motions. That's about all I can say for it. This living at contract hotels isn't eating; it isn't even feeding. You folks back with the show don't have to put up with contract hotels; you eat under the cook tent and you get real food."

"What's a contract hotel?" asked Teddy.

Phil looked at his companion in disgust.

"Teddy Tucker, haven't you been in the show business long enough to know what a contract hotel is?"

Teddy shook his head.

"I'll tell you, I'll explain what a contract hotel is," said Billy. "The contracting agent goes over the route in the spring and makes the arrangements for the show. He engages the livery rigs to take the men out on the country routes, and when he gets through with the livery stable business he hunts up all the almost food places in town until he finds one that will feed the advance car men for five or ten cents a meal. Then he signs a contract and goes off to a real hotel for his own meal. Oh, no, Mr. Contracting Agent doesn't get his meals there. Well, we're booked to eat at one of those almost food places in every town we make. And some of them are not even 'almost.' We are going to one of the kind now. Want to come along?"

"Sure," replied Teddy.

"You won't be so anxious after you have had a week or so of them."

All hands started for the hotel.

"What about your reports? I thought Mr. Snowden told you to get them in at once," asked Phil after they had left the car.

"Let him wait," growled Billy.

"But he will raise a row when you get back, will he not?"

"He'll roar anyway, so what's the odds? We're used to that."

"A queer business, this advance car work," said Phil thoughtfully. "I never had any idea that it was like this. If ever I own or run a show it will be different--I mean the advance cars will be run on a different principle from this one."

"I hope you do, and that I am working for you," grinned Conley. "Here we are."

Billy's description of a contract hotel Phil decided had not been overdrawn. All hands filed into the dining room, and Phil had lost most of his appetite before reaching his chair.

A waiter who looked as if he might have been a prizefighter at one time shambled up to them with a soiled napkin thrown over one arm. As it chanced, he approached Teddy first.

"Bean soup! What'll you have," he demanded with a suddenness that startled the Circus Boy.

Teddy surveyed the waiter with large eyes, then permitted his gaze to wander about the table to the faces of the grinning billposters.

"Bean soup. What'll I have?" reflected the lad soberly. "Now isn't it funny that I can't think what kind of soup I want. Bean soup; what'll I have?"

The waiter shifted his weight to the other foot, flopped the napkin to the other arm and stuck out his chin belligerently.

"Bean soup! What'll you have?" he demanded, with a rising inflection in his voice.

"Let me think. Why, I guess I'll take bean soup if it's all the same to you," decided Tucker, solemn as an owl.

The billposters broke out into a roar of laughter. They fairly howled with delight at Teddy's droll manner, but the Circus Boy did not even smile. He looked at them with a hurt expression in his eyes until the men were on the point of apologizing to him.

They did not know young Tucker.

The rest of the meal passed off without incident.

"Well, what did you think of the contract hotel?" questioned Conley, as they were strolling back to the car.

"I think I shall starve to death in a week, if I have to eat in that sort of a place," answered Teddy. "Why didn't the contracting agent sign us up with a livery stable? I'd a sight rather feed there than at a contract hotel if they are all like this."

"Yes, the food is at least clean in a livery stable," laughed Phil. "But we shall get along all right. If we get too hungry we can go out and buy our own meals now and then. Do you ever do that, Mr. Conley?"

"I should say we do. We have to, or we shouldn't have any stomachs left. Now, you want to know something about this car work, don't you?"

"I should like to very much, if you can spare the time to tell me about it."

"Wait till I get my report made out, then we'll have a nice long talk, and I will tell you all about it."

"There is Mr. Snowden waiting for you."

"Never mind him. His bite isn't half so bad as his bark."

The men piled into the car, whereupon Manager Snowden unloosed the vials of his wrath because their reports were not in. To his tirade no one gave the slightest heed. The men went methodically to work, writing out their reports to which they signed their names, folded the papers, and tossed them on the manager's desk without a word of explanation.

For a few moments there was silence in the office while the manager was going over the reports. All at once there was a roar.

"Pig! Come here!"

Rosie got down from the pile of paper on which he had been sitting, taking his time about doing so, and, wearing a broad grin, strolled to the office at the other end of the car.

"What's the trouble now?" demanded Rosie.

"Trouble? Trouble? That's the word. It's trouble all the time. Where are your brains?"

"In my head, I suppose," grinned Rosie.

"No!" thundered the manager. "They're in your feet. All you know how to do is to kick. You're a woodenhead; you're no good."

Rosie accepted the tirade with a quiet smile.

"If you will tell me what it is all about I may be able to explain."

"Look at those billboard tickets!"

"What's the matter with them?"

"Matter? Matter?"

"Yes, that's what I asked."

"They're torn off crooked."

"Well, what of that?"

"What of that? Why, you woodenhead, when those tickets are presented at the door when the show comes around, the ticket takers won't accept them. Then there will be a howl that you can hear all across the state of Minnesota. How many times have I told you to be careful?"

"The tickets are all right," growled Rosie, now a little nettled.

"What! What! You dare contradict me? I'll fire you Saturday night! I'd fire you now only I am short of money. Get out of here! Come back!"

Rosie turned dutifully, but with a weary expression on his face.

"I fine you eleven dollars and fifty cents. That's about what the tickets will come to. Now go. Send Rain-in-the-Face here!"

The interview with Rain-in-the-Face sounded not unlike a series of explosions to those out in the main compartment of the car. Every face wore a grin, and each man expected it would be his turn next.

"Come on, let's go outside and talk," said Conley.

"I should think you **would** want to get away from it all," answered Phil. "I don't know; whether I can stand this sort of thing or not."

"You'll get used to it after awhile."

"Something's going to happen," croaked the Missing Link, dismally, as the two left the car by the rear door.

"I guess the freak is right," nodded Billy Conley. "There is going to be an explosion here that will shake the state."

There was, but not exactly in the way he imagined.

CHAPTER V
THE MIDNIGHT ALARM

Now tell me, if you will, what the routine of the work on an advance car is," said Phil after he and Billy had sat down beside the tracks.

"It would take all night to do that, but I'll give you a few pointers and the rest you will have to pick up for yourself. In the first place an advertising car includes billposters, lithographers, banner men and at least one programmer."

"Sounds all right, but it doesn't mean much of anything to me," laughed Phil.

"The billposters post the large bills on the billboards, and anywhere else that they can get a chance, mostly out in the country and in the country towns. In places where there is a regular billposter, he does that work for us. Any boards not owned by a billposter, or a barn or a pigpen or a henhouse on the road is called a 'daub.' At least two tickets are given for every place we put a piece of paper on. These tickets are numbered and signed. Now, if a fellow out in Kankakee, we will say, should chance to tear down the bill, when he presented his ticket at the gate on the day of the show, it would be refused. He'd pay or stay out."

"But how would they know he had taken down the poster," questioned Phil.

"Checkers follow along at intervals and check up every piece of paper we put up. We send the record of our work to the car back of us and they in turn send our and their reports to the car behind them."

"It is a wonderful system, indeed," marveled Phil.

"Yes. To go back a little I will say that this is a 'scout car' or what is known among showmen as 'the opposition car.' It goes only where there is trouble, where there is opposition. For instance, more than half a dozen shows are coming into this territory, this season, and it is up to us to cover every available space with our paper before their cars get on the ground."

"But will they not paste their bills over yours, over those you have already put up?"

"They seldom do. It is an unwritten law in the show business that this is not to be done."

Teddy had come up to them in time to hear the last remark.

"I thought there wasn't any law, written or unwritten, in this business," he said.

"You will find there is, young man. Then, to come to the lithographers, as I think I already have told you, these men place small bills in store and shop windows, giving tickets for the privilege the same as do the billposters. One man goes ahead of them and does what we call 'the squaring,' meaning that he enters the stores and asks the privilege of putting up the lithographs. In most cases the owners of the places object, and he has to convince them that it is to their advantage to have the paper in their windows."

"I didn't think there was so much to it, but I think I should like that work. I'll be a squarer," decided Teddy.

"The banner men put up what are called 'banners,' cloth signs. These are tacked up in high places and the banner men have to be good climbers. They fill their mouths with tacks, points in, heads out. They use magnetic hammers."

"What's this, a joke?" interrupted Teddy.

"It is not a joke. The head of each hammer so used is a magnet, and is used to pick the tacks from the mouth of the banner man. The tack sticks to the head of the hammer and is thus ready to be driven. An expert banner man will drive tacks almost as rapidly as you could fire a self-acting revolver."

"That is odd. What does the fellow called the programmer do?"

"He takes the small printed matter around, and drops it on doorsteps and in stores. When we are making a day run with the car he drops the printed matter off at stations and crossroads, or wherever he sees a man. Following us come route-riders."

"What are they?"

"Men who ride over the country routes to see whether the billposters have put up the paper indicated on their reports, or thrown the stuff in a ditch somewhere. After them come checkers, one after the other. This is Car Three, as you know. Car

Two follows about two weeks behind us, and Car One comes along a week ahead of the show. What are you going to do?"

"Mr. Snowden said I was to go out with one of the men on a country route."

"Then you come along with me, unless he directs you differently. I can give you pointers that would take you a long time to learn were you left to pick them up yourself. Don't say anything to him about it unless he speaks to you, but prepare to go out with me early in the morning. I have a big drive tomorrow, some fifty miles, and you will get all you want for one day's work."

"Yes; that will be fine."

"What is your friend here to do?"

"I am the paste-maker," answered Teddy with a sheepish grin. "I make the stickum stuff for this outfit."

"A nice job," jeered the assistant manager. "You will get all you want of that work in about thirty minutes. The Boss must certainly have a grudge against you. You will be hanging around the car all day, however, and if the Boss is away any you will have a chance to get forty winks of sleep in the stateroom now and then."

"No; Teddy is not here to sleep. He is here to work."

"Yes; everybody works around here but Father."

"Is the work the same on the advance cars of all shows?"

"All circuses, yes. We do things just the same as the fellows did them forty years ago. Nobody seems to have head enough to do things differently, and goodness knows some modern methods are necessary."

"How long have you been on this car?"

"Four years; this is my fifth season here."

"Why, that is exactly the time we have been with the Sparling Shows."

Billy nodded.

"I saw you work last season. You are a bird on the trapeze, and ride--whew, but you can beat anything I ever saw on bareback! I knew I had seen you before when you came in this evening, but I couldn't place you. I remembered after a little. Say, Phil, I'm glad you handed it out to the Boss this afternoon."

"And I am very sorry. I don't know what Mr. Sparling will think of it. Still, I had to do something. I saw right away that he had made up his mind to treat us badly. What time do we pull out tonight?"

"Twelve o'clock, I think. And speaking of that, it is time to turn in."

The three entered the car. Mr. Snowden already had turned in, his end of the car being dark and silent. Most of the billposters also had climbed to their berths near the roof of the car, and some of them were snoring heavily.

"Do they do this all night long?" questioned Teddy.

"Do what?"

"Roll logs!"

"Well, yes," laughed Billy; "they are pretty good snorers, all of them. Do you snore?"

"I might, on a pinch. I don't know whether I do or not. I am usually asleep when I snore. How about it, Phil, do I snore?"

"Not when I am within punching distance of you."

The boys undressed, got into their pajamas, and after considerable effort managed to climb to the top of the pile of paper, where their blankets had been spread for them by the porter.

"Not much of a bed, is it Teddy?" laughed Phil.

"The worst ever!" agreed Teddy. "How I'm going to stick in that bed when the car gets under motion I don't know. I wish I was back with the show."

"Never mind, old chap. We have had things pretty easy for the last four years. A little hardship will not hurt either of us. And I know we are going to like this life, after we get more used to it. What time do we get up; do you know?"

"No, I don't know anything about it. I guess in time for late breakfast," answered Teddy grimly. "Good night."

In a few minutes the Circus Boys were sound asleep. They did not even awaken when, about midnight, a switch engine hooked to their car, and after racing them up and down the railroad yards a few times, coupled them to the rear of the passenger train that was to pull them to their next stand, some seventy-five miles away. A few minutes later and they were rolling away. The road was a crooked one and the car swayed dizzily, but they were too used to the sensation to be in the least disturbed by it.

An hour or two had passed when, all at once, every man in the car was suddenly startled by a blood-curdling yell and a wild commotion somewhere in the darkness of the car.

"What is it?"

"Are we wrecked?"

"What did we hit?"

This and other exclamations were shouted in loud tones, as the men came tumbling from their berths, some sprawling over the floor, where a lurch of the car had hurled them.

CHAPTER VI
ALMOST A TRAGEDY

Strike a light!"

"Are we off the rails?"

"No, you idiot. Don't you feel the car going just the same as before? And he's wheeling her a mile a minute at that. Hurry with that light, somebody!" commanded Billy.

At this moment they heard the sliding door of the manager's stateroom come open with a crash.

"Now, here's trouble for certain!" muttered the Missing Link. "The Boss is on deck."

"I guess my friend Teddy has got into trouble," said Phil Forrest, slipping quickly from his bed on top of a pile of gaudy circus posters. "Ted! Ted, where are you?"

There was no answer.

"What is all this row about?" thundered the manager, stalking down the car, clad only in his pajamas.

"We do not know, sir. We are trying to find out. I am afraid my friend has fallen out of bed and hurt himself," answered Phil.

"I hope it killed him!" bellowed Mr. Snowden. "The idea of waking up the whole car at this time of the night! This nonsense has got to stop, and right quick at that. Where's that light?"

Phil was groping about the floor, trying hurriedly to locate Teddy. But no Teddy was to be found.

Finally a match flickered; after lurching about the car the man with the match finally succeeded in locating the bracket lamp near the end of the car.

Anxious eyes peered about them in the dim light.

"Look!" howled Rosie the Pig.

A pair of wildly kicking legs were seen protruding from one of the big paste cans, these cans being made like the big garbage cans that one sees in backyards in the city.

"It's Teddy! There he is!" cried Phil, springing forward.

"He's gone in the paste can head first!" yelled another of the crew.

"Help me get him out; he has stuck fast!" shouted Phil, tugging desperately at his companion's heels.

The car set up a roar of laughter at the ludicrous sight. To Phil, however, it was no laughing matter. The paste can was nearly full of paste and of about the same consistency as dough in a bread pan. It was thick and wickedly blue, for it had been mixed with bluestone to preserve it until required by the billposters.

"Pull him out, you idiots!" bellowed the car manager. "If he isn't dead now, he can't be killed. Pull him out and throw him overboard!"

Phil flashed an indignant look at Mr. Snowden.

By this time others had come to his assistance. It required their united efforts to rescue Teddy from his perilous predicament.

They hauled him out and laid him on the door.

"Teddy, Teddy!" cried Phil, but Tucker made no reply. In the first place his mouth was so full of paste that he could not utter a sound. Again, he was half unconscious, nearly smothered and still unable to breathe freely.

Phil grabbed off the jacket of his own pajamas and began wiping the blue paste from the unfortunate lad's mouth, eyes and nose.

A happy thought appeared to strike the car manager. He dashed to the sink, and, quickly filling a pail of water, ran back to the spot where Teddy was lying.

Snowden turned the pail bottom side up, apparently intending to douse the water into Tucker's face.

Instead, the contents of the pail landed on Phil Forrest's head, spreading itself over his bare back, and trickled down in rivulets over Teddy's face.

The water was almost ice cold.

"Wow!" howled Phil, springing to his feet. "Who did that?"

"I did, and I'll do it again," jeered the car manager.

"Get me another pail, but I'll do the spilling this time. Don't you dare duck me again, or I'll settle with you after I get through with my friend."

One of the crew grabbed up the pail to run for water. This time the pail was handed to Phil who instantly began mopping the face of young Tucker.

In a moment or so Teddy began to gasp. His dive had nearly been the end of him.

"Get a net," he murmured as he slowly came to, whereat everyone save the car manager laughed loudly. "Wha--what happened? Did we run off the track?"

"No, you took a high dive into a can of paste," jeered Billy. "You're the champion high diver of Car Three."

Mr. Snowden, stooping over, grabbed the luckless Teddy by the collar and jerked him to his feet.

"Get up, you lummox!" he commanded.

Teddy blinked very fast. Mr. Snowden began to shake him. Phil stepped forward quickly and pushed the car manager away.

"Wha--what!" growled Snowden, an angry light leaping into his eyes.

"You let the boy alone," commanded Phil. "Because he has had an accident is no reason why you should punish him!"

"You--you--you--"

Phil paid no heed to him, but led the unsteady Teddy to the far end of the compartment.

"You get off this car, both of you!" yelled the manager.

"What, with the train running sixty miles an hour?" questioned Phil, turning slowly.

"Yes; I don't care if it kills you both. Good riddance--good job if it did."

"I think you have another guess coming, Mr. Car Manager," replied Phil calmly.

Snowden glared at the Circus Boy who had thus defied him; then turning sharply on his bare heel he strode back to his stateroom.

A broad grin appeared on the faces of the car crew.

"I guess that will be about all for this evening," announced Rain-in-the-Face.

"Is there a rope on this car?" asked Phil.

"Yes; what do you want a rope for?" replied Billy.

"He's going to complete the job by hanging the Boss from a brake beam," spoke up Rosie.

"Not quite as bad as that, I guess," laughed Phil. "I am going to tie my friend Teddy in his bed. There is no telling what may happen to him, if I do not. Teddy, had we happened to be sound sleepers you would in all probability be dead by this time."

Tucker shivered.

"That would please Mr. Snowden too much, you know."

"Then tie me in. I don't want to please him. Did he duck me while I was asleep?"

"He tried to. As it chanced my bare back got most of the ducking," answered Phil with a short laugh, for he believed the car manager had purposely poured the water on him.

"But he shook me," protested Teddy.

"He did that," chorused the crew. "What are you going to do about it?"

"Well," reflected Tucker; "I think he and I will fight a duel tomorrow at sunrise."

Once more all hands turned in, Phil humorously making a pretense of tying his companion to his "berth." As a matter of fact, Phil did tie the rope about Teddy's wrist, wrapping the free end about his own arm, and thus the boys went to sleep once more.

It seemed as if they had been asleep only a few minutes when they were suddenly startled into wakefulness by a loud noise.

This time, however, it was not a yell, but a roar.

Phil sat up suddenly, rubbing his eyes sleepily.

"Get up, you lazy good-for-nothings!" bellowed the car manager, dancing up and down the aisle, still in his pajamas, his hair standing up, his eyes wild and menacing.

"Is that all?" muttered Teddy, sinking back into a sound sleep again.

Phil sprang from the pile of papers on which he had been sleeping, landing lightly on the floor in his bare feet.

"Good morning, Mr. Snowden. I hope you had a good night's sleep," greeted the Circus Boy.

Snowden glared at the lad, as if trying to make up his mind whether or not Phil was making sport of him. But there was only pleasantness in the face of Phil

Forrest.

"Huh!" grunted the manager. Then he once more began racing up and down the car, roaring at his men, threatening and expressing his opinion of them in the way with which Phil already had become familiar.

Teddy lay curled up, with one foot protruding from beneath the covers. Whether or not he had done this purposely, it was difficult to decide. Be that as it may, Mr. Snowden caught sight of the pink foot. He rose to the bait like a bass to a fly.

In another second he had pounced upon the foot. Grabbing it with both hands he gave it a violent tug. Tucker responded. He came slipping from the "berth," throwing the quilts before him as he did so. The quilts landed over the car manager's head. Then came Teddy Tucker.

Ted landed, full on Mr. Snowden's head, with a wild yell.

Down went the manager and the Circus Boy, with the latter on top, in a writhing, howling, confused heap.

CHAPTER VII
THE FIRST DAY'S EXPERIENCE

Give it to him, Teddy!" howled the crew.

Tucker, as soon as he could right himself, sat down on the manager's head, at the same time holding Mr. Snowden's hands pinioned to the floor.

The muffled voice under the quilts waxed louder and more angry as the seconds passed. Phil, who had gone to the wash room to make his toilet, hurried back at sound of the row.

"Teddy Tucker, what are you doing?" demanded Phil, for the moment puzzled at the scene before him.

"I'm sitting on the Boss," answered Teddy triumphantly. "Shall I give him one for you?"

"Yes--give him two for each of us," shouted the billposters.

Phil strode to his companion, grabbed the lad by the collar of his pajamas and jerked him from the helpless man under the quilts.

"Now, you behave yourself, young man, or you will have to reckon with me," he commanded, pushing Teddy aside.

"You let me alone. This is my inning. I guess I can sit on the Boss, if I want to, without your interfering with the fun."

Giving no heed to the words, Phil quickly hauled the quilts off and assisted Mr. Snowden to rise.

"I guess Teddy must have fallen on you, sir," suggested Phil solemnly.

"He did it on purpose! He did it on purpose!"

"You pulled him out of bed, did you not, sir?"

"Yes; and next time I'll pull him so he'll know it. Get out of here, every man of you, and get your breakfasts; then get off on your routes. Things are coming to a fine pass on this car. Young man, I will talk to you later."

The manager, with red face and angry eye, strode to his stateroom, while the grinning billposters made haste to get into their clothes. A few minutes later, and all hands were on their way to breakfast.

This meal at the new hotel was a slight improvement over the dinner they had eaten the night before. Besides, all hands were in good humor, for they had had more real excitement on Car Three, since the advent of the Circus Boys, than at any time during the season.

By the time they reached the car again six livery teams were in waiting for the men who were to go out on the country routes.

All was instantly bustle and excitement. Paste cans were loaded into the wagons, brushes and pails, together with the paper that had been carefully laid out and counted, the night before, for each billposter. A record of this was kept on the car.

Phil lent a hand at loading the stuff, and they found that the slim lad was stronger than any of them. It was an easy matter for him to lift one of the big cans of paste to a wagon without assistance. Teddy, however, stood by with hands thrust in pockets, an amused grin on his face. The baleful eye of the car manager was upon him.

"Have you heard from Mr. Sparling this morning?" asked Phil.

"Yes," answered Mr. Snowden shortly.

"What did he say?"

"That is none of your business, young man."

"You are right. I accept the rebuke. While I am interested, it really is none of my business," answered the lad with a smile.

"Where are you going?"

"You told me to go out on one of the country routes."

"Oh! What route are you going on, if I may ask?"

"I had thought of going with Mr. Conley."

"You will do nothing of the sort. You will go where I tell you to. I--"

"I suggested that he go with me, Mr. Snowden," interposed Billy. "I have a hard route to work today and I shall need some help if I get over it before dark."

"Very well; go on. I hope he falls off a barn or something. If he does, leave him."

"For your sake, I shall try to take care of myself," answered Phil with an encouraging smile.

"Tucker!"

"Yes, sir."

"Start a fire under that boiler. Henry, you show him how to manage the boiler and mix the paste. I don't imagine he even knows dough when he sees it."

"I know a dough-head when I see one," spoke up Teddy promptly, after delivering himself of which sentiment he strolled away with hands in his pockets, whistling merrily.

The drive to the country in the fresh morning air was a most delightful one to Phil. After leaving the town they soon came in sight of a deserted house. It evidently had been abandoned, for it was in a bad state of dilapidation.

"There's a dandy daub!" exclaimed Billy. "We'll plaster it with paper until the neighbors won't know it. When we get there, hop off and bring some pails of water, will you?"

"Sure," answered Phil. While he was doing this, the billposter was spreading his paper out on the ground, deciding on the layout that he would post.

A few minutes later and the gaudy bills were going up like magic on the road side of the house and the two ends, so that the pictures might be seen from every point of view from the highway. The house had been transformed into a blaze of color.

"All right," sang out Billy. "Good job, too."

Phil had learned something. He had noted every movement of the billposter.

"How long does it take to learn to post, Billy?" he asked.

"Some fellows never learn. Others get fairly expert after a few weeks puttering around."

"May I try one today?"

"Sure thing. If the next one is easy I will give you a chance at it."

The next daub proved to be a small hay barn a little way back in a field.

"There's your chance, my boy," he said.

Phil jumped out before the wagon had come to a stop and, with paper and brush under his arms, ran across the field. With more skill than might have been expected with his limited experience he smeared the paper with paste, then sought to raise it up to the side of the building as he had seen Billy Conley do.

This was where Phil came to grief. A gust of wind doubled the paper up, the pasted side smearing the bright colors of the face of the picture, until the colors were one hopeless daub. To cap the climax the whole thing came down over Phil's head, wrapping him in its slimy folds.

"Hey, help!" he shouted. "I'm posting myself instead of the barn."

Billy sat down on the ground, laughing until the tears ran down his cheeks.

"If it hadn't been for that unexpected gust of wind I should have made it nicely," explained Phil with a sickly grin. "Oh, pshaw, I'm not as much of a billposters as I thought I was. I guess there is more to this game than I had any idea of."

"You will learn. You took a pretty big contract when you tried to put up that eight-sheet."

"We will let you try a one-sheet on the farther end of the barn. A one-sheet is a small, twenty-eight inch piece of paper, you know."

Phil nodded.

"I'll try it," he said. "I guess a one-sheet is about as big a piece of paper as I am fit to handle just yet."

He managed the one-sheet without the least trouble, and did a very good job, so much so that Billy complimented him highly.

"You will make a billposter yet. One good thing about you is that you are willing to learn, and you are quick to admit that you do not know it all. Most fellows, when they start, have ideas of their own--at least they think they have."

After that Phil did the small work, thinned the paste and made himself generally useful.

"Oh, look at that!" he cried, pointing off ahead of them.

"What is it, Phil?"

"See that building standing up on that high piece of ground. Wouldn't that be a dandy place on which to post some paper?"

The building he had indicated was a tall circular structure, painted a dark red, with a small cupola effect crowning its top.

"That is a silo. You wouldn't be able to get permission to post a bill on there, even if you could get up there to do it," said Conley.

"Why not?"

"Why not? Why that farmer, I'll wager, sets as much store by that building as he does his newly-painted house."

"I'll go ask him. You don't mind if I 'square' him, do you?" questioned the lad with a twinkle in his eyes.

"Ask him, for sure. But we couldn't post up there. We have no ladders that would reach; in fact we have no ladders at all. I mean the farmer has no ladders long enough."

"Never mind; I'll figure out a way," replied the Circus Boy, whose active mind already had decided upon a method by which he thought he might accomplish the feat, providing the farmer was willing.

Reaching the farm, Phil jumped out and ran up to the house.

"Do you own this place, sir?" he asked of the farmer who answered his ring at the bell.

"I do."

"It's a beautiful place. I am representing the Sparling Circus, and we thought we would like to make a display on your silo."

The farmer gazed at him in amazement.

"Young man, you have a cast-iron nerve even to ask such a thing."

"I know the mere matter of tickets to the show will be no inducement to a man of your position. But I am going to make you a present of a box for six people at the circus. You will take your whole family and be my guest. I will not only give you an order for it, but will write a personal letter to the owner, who is my very good friend. He will show you all there is to be seen, and I will see to it that you take dinner with him in the circus tent. No; there is no obligation. All the farmers--all your neighbors will be envious. I want you to come. We won't speak of the silo. I don't expect you to let me post that; but, if you will permit me to put a three-sheet on your hog pen back there, I shall be greatly obliged."

Despite the farmer's protestations, Phil wrote out the order for the box, then scribbled a few lines to Mr. Sparling, which he enclosed in an envelope borrowed from the farmer.

"Thank you so much," beamed the Circus Boy, handing over the letter to the farmer, accompanied by the pass and order for the arena box at the circus. "It is a pleasure to meet a man like you. I come from a country town myself, and have worked some on my uncle's farm."

"You with the circus, eh?"

"Yes, sir."

"Looks to me like you was a pretty young fellow to be a circus man."

"Oh no, not very. I belong back with the show. I am a performer, you know. I am out with the advertising car to learn the business."

"A performer?" wondered the farmer, looking over the trim figure and bright boyish face. "What do you perform?"

"I perform on the flying trapeze and do a bareback riding act."

"Is that so?"

"Yes, sir."

"Do you know, young fellow, I never got such a close squint at a circus fellow before in my life. But, come to size you up, I reckon you can do all them things you've been telling me about. Yes, sir, I'll go to the circus. Will you be there to cut up in the ring?"

"I cannot say. It is doubtful, as I probably shall be ahead of the show for the rest of the season. Well, thank you very much. We will decorate the hog pen," added the lad, touching his cap and turning away.

An arena box, value twelve dollars, was a pretty high price to pay for a three-sheet on a hog pen, but Phil Forrest knew what he was doing. At least he thought he did, and he did not walk very fast on his way to the road.

"Hey, come back here," called the farmer.

"Yes, sir," answered Phil turning inquiringly.

"Come here."

He walked back to where the farmer was standing fingering the pass and the letter.

"I--I reckon you needn't stick them bills on the hog pen."

The Circus Boy's heart took a sudden drop.

"Very well, sir; just as you say. I do not wish to do anything to displease you."

"But I reckon you can plaster that silo full of them circus pictures from top to bottom, if you want to," was the unexpected announcement.

Phil Forrest's heart bounded back into position again.

CHAPTER VIII
THE CIRCUS BOY WINS

O h, thank you, thank you ever so much!" answered the lad, his eyes glowing.

"You're a square kid and I like you."

"I appreciate your kindness, I assure you, and I will write a letter to the owner of the show about you this evening when I get back to the car. Have you any ladders that we can borrow, and a long rope?"

"I reckon you'll find all them things in the hay barn. Help yourself. I've got to run up to the back farm, but maybe I'll be back before you get through your job. So long."

Phil hurried back to the road, where Billy and the wagon were waiting. The lad's feet felt lighter than usual.

"Well, what luck?" demanded Billy.

"I may be a poor apology as a billposter, but as a diplomat I'm a winner, Billy."

"You--you don't mean you got the silo?" gasped Conley.

"I got the silo, and I can have the hog pen too, if I want it, and perhaps the farmer's house thrown in for good measure," answered Phil, his face flushed from his first triumph as a publicity showman.

"Well, of all the nerve!"

"That's what the farmer said," laughed Phil. "But he changed his mind."

"What do you think of that?" demanded Billy, turning to the driver.

"The kid is all right."

"You're right; he is. The next question, now that you have got the silo, is what are you going to do with it?"

"Post it," answered Phil promptly.

"You can never do it."

"I'll show you what a circus man can do."

"Come along and unload your truck. Help me get some ladders out of the barn."

Wonderingly, Billy did as he was bid, and the driver, now grown interested, hitched his horses to the fence and followed them.

The silo was empty. Phil measured the distance to the top with his eyes.

"About forty feet I should say," he decided. "We shall have to do some climbing."

The ladders were far too short, but by splicing two of them together, they reached up to an opening in the silo some ten feet from the top.

Phil hunted about until he found a long plank; then setting the spliced ladders up inside the silo he mounted to the opening, carrying one end of a coil of rope with him. Upon reaching the opening he directed Billy to tie the other end of the rope to the plank. This being done, Phil hauled the board up to where he was sitting perched on the frame of the opening.

"I'd like to know what you're going to do?"

"If you will come up here I will show you."

"Not on your life," replied Billy promptly. "I know when I'm well off, and if you don't look out, Boss Snowden will get his wish."

"What wish was that?"

"That you might fall off a barn and break your neck."

The Circus Boy's merry laugh floated down to them as he worked in an effort to get the plank into position. By tying the rope to one end of the plank to support it he gradually worked the plank out through the opening, after a time managing to shove the end nearest to him under a beam.

"There, I'd like to see you turn a trick like that, Billy Conley," he shouted.

"*I* wouldn't," retorted Billy. "What's the next move?"

"In a minute. Watch me!"

The lad made a large loop in the rope in the shape of a slip knot. All preparations being made he boldly walked out on the plank which, secured at one end like a springboard, bent and trembled beneath his weight.

The men down below gasped.

The farmer, having changed his mind, had come out to watch the operation rather than visit the back farm. Two neighbors had by this time joined him.

"Who's the fellow up there?" asked one.

"He is a performer in a circus."

"A performer? Shucks! He's no more performer than I am."

"Watch him and perhaps you may change your mind," answered Billy, who had overheard the remark. "That boy is one of the finest circus performers in this country. Do you think he could stand out on that plank, more than thirty feet above the ground, if he were not a performer? Why, I wouldn't be up there for a million dollars, and you wouldn't, either."

"That's right," answered the farmer himself. "That beats all the circus performances I ever saw. What is the kid going to do?"

"I don't know," confessed Billy. "He knows and that's enough."

Phil, having tested the plank to his satisfaction and studied his balance, now cast his eyes up to the little cupola on top of the silo. Then he began slowly swinging the loop of the rope over his head, after the fashion of a cowboy about to make a cast.

They were at a loss to understand what he was trying to do, but every man there was sure in his own mind what Phil Forrest would do--fall off.

Suddenly he let go of the loop. It soared upward. Then they began to understand. He was trying to rope the cupola.

The rope fell short by about three feet, as nearly as he was able to judge.

"Oh, pshaw!" muttered Phil. "That was a clumsy throw. I would make just about as good a cowboy as I am a billposters. Well, here goes for another try."

He put all his strength into the throw this time.

The rope sped true, dropping as neatly over the peak of the cupola as if the thrower had been standing directly over the projection.

A cheer rose from the men below.

It died on their lips.

"He's falling!" they cried with one voice.

The farmers stood gaping. But Billy, with the quick instincts of a showman, darted beneath the plank hoping to catch and break the lad's fall.

Phil had leaned too far backward in making his cast. He had lost his balance and toppled over. Here his training in aerial work served him in good stead. As he felt himself going he turned quickly facing toward the outer end of the plank.

Like a flash both hands shot out. They closed about the end of the plank by a desperately narrow margin.

The plank bent until it seemed as if it must snap under his weight. Then it shot upward, carrying the boy with it, he kicking his feet together as he was lifted and laughing out of pure bravado.

Phil knew he was safe now. The drop had tested the plank, so that there was now slight danger of its breaking.

On the second rebound he swung himself to the upper side of it and stood up.

"Hurrah!" he shouted.

Billy was pale and trembling.

"If you do that again I'll have an attack of heart disease, Phil!" he called. "Now, what are you going to do? The rope is hanging seven or eight feet away from you."

"Hello, that's so. I hadn't observed that before. I should not have let go of it. Never mind, I'll get it unless something breaks. See here, Billy, you get from under there."

"Is the plank likely to fall?" asked Billy innocently.

"The plank? No. I am likely to take a tumble," answered Phil, with a short laugh. All at once he grew serious and still. "I think I can make it," he decided.

His resolution formed, the lad crouched low, so as not to throw so great a leverage on the plank that it would slip from under him when he leaped. He prepared for the spring.

"Don't do it!" howled Billy, now thoroughly frightened. "Don't you see what he's up to? He's going to jump off the plank and try to catch hold of the rope hanging from the cupola. He'll never make it. He'll miss it sure as he's a foot high. This is awful!"

"Don't bother me, Billy. Mr. Farmer, is that cupola strong enough to bear my weight on a sudden jolt?"

"It ought to hold a ton, dead weight."

"Then I guess it will hold me. Don't talk to me down there. Here goes!"

It seemed a foolhardy thing to do. To the average person it would have meant almost sure death. It must be remembered, however, that Phil Forrest was a circus performer, that he felt as thoroughly at home far above the ground as he did when standing directly on it.

He leaped out into the air, cleared the intervening space between the plank and the rope, his fingers closing over the latter with a sureness born of long experience.

His body swung far over toward the other side of the silo, settling down with a sickening jolt, as the loop over the cupola slipped down tight.

"Hooray!" cried Phil, twisting the rope about one leg and waving a hand to those below him.

They drew a long, relieved sigh. The farmers, one after the other, took off their hats and mopped their foreheads.

"Warm, isn't it?" grinned the owner of the silo.

"Now, pass up your brush and paste on this rope." Phil had brought a small rope with him for this very purpose.

Billy got busy at once and in a few minutes Phil had the brush and paste in his hands, with which he proceeded to smear as much of the side of the silo as was within reach. It will be remembered that he was hanging on the rope by one leg, around which the rope was twisted as only showmen know how to do.

"Now, the paper," called Phil.

This was passed up to him in the same way. In a few moments he had pasted on a great sheet, having first pulled himself up to the eaves to secure the top of the sheet just under them.

"Now that you have one sheet on, how are you going to get around to the other side to put others on?" demanded Conley.

"Oh, I'll show you. Be patient down there. I have got to change a leg; this one is getting numb."

"I should think it would," muttered Billy.

Phil changed legs, as he termed it; then, grasping the eaves with both hands, he pulled himself along, the slip-noose over the cupola turning about on its pivot without a hitch.

This done Phil called for more paper, which was put up in short order. Thus he continued with his work until he had put a plaster, as Bill Conley characterized it, all the way around the farmer's silo. It might have been seen nearly ten miles away in all directions. No such billing had ever before been done in that part of the country, nor perhaps anywhere else.

"There! I'd like to see the Ringlings, or Hagenbecks or Barnum and Bailey or any of the other big ones, beat that. They're welcome to cover this paper if they can, eh, Billy?" laughed Phil, pushing himself away from the side of the silo and leaning far back to get a better view of it. "I call that pretty fine. How about it?"

"The greatest ever," agreed Billy. His vocabulary was too limited to express his thoughts fully, but he did fairly well with what he had.

Having satisfied himself that his work was well done, Phil let himself down slowly, not using his hands at all, in doing so, but taking a spiral course downward.

"H-u-m-m, I'm a little stiff," he said when his feet touched the ground. "Am I a billposter or am I not a billposter, Billy?"

"You are the champeen of 'em all! I take off my hat to you." Which Conley did, then and there.

"I am afraid I shall not be able to get that rope down, sir," said Phil politely to the farmer. "I am sorry. I had not figured on that before. If you will be good enough to tell me how much the rope is worth I shall be glad to pay you for it. I can cut it off up near the little door there, so it will not look quite so bad. Shall I do it?"

"No. You needn't bother. As for paying for the rope I won't take a cent. I've had more fun than the price of a dozen ropes could buy. Why, young man, do you know I never seen anything in a circus that could touch the outside edge of the performance you've been giving us this afternoon? You boys had your dinners?"

"No," confessed the Circus Boy. "I guess we had forgotten all about eating."

"Then come right in the house. My wife will get you something, and I want to introduce her to a real live circus man--that's you."

"Thank you."

Phil's eyes were bright. He was happy in the accomplishment of a piece of work that was not done every day. In fact, this one was destined to go down in show history as a remarkable achievement.

They sat down to a fine dinner, and Phil entertained the family for an hour relating his experiences in the show world.

When the hour came for leaving, the farmer urged them to remain, but the men had work to do and a long drive ahead of them.

They drove away, Phil waving his hat and the farmer and his wife waving hat and apron respectively.

As the rig reached a hill, some three miles away, Phil and Billy turned to survey their work.

"Looks like a fire, doesn't it, Billy?"

"It sure does. It would call out the fire department if there was one here."

"And the best of it is, that posting will be up there when the show comes this way next season. It is a standing advertisement for the Great Sparling Shows. But I suppose Mr. Snowden would say it wasn't much of a job."

CHAPTER IX
TEDDY GETS INTO TROUBLE

G et those paste cans outside! Step lively there!"

"Say, you talk to me as if I were one of the hired help," objected Teddy, his face flushing.

"Well, that is exactly what you are. You'll soon learn that you are hired help if you remain on this car. I'll take all the freshness out of you. The flour is in the cellar."

"In the cellar?"

"That's what I said. Go down and get it out. You will require about a sack and a half for each can. That will be about right for a can of paste. Henry will show you how much bluestone to put in. But be careful of that boiler. I don't want the car blown up."

The manager strode away to his office, while Teddy, red and perspiring, went about his work. He was much more meek than usual, and this very fact, had the manager known him better, would have impressed Mr. Snowden as a suspicious circumstance.

Instead of the usual pink tights with spangled trunks, Teddy Tucker was now clad in a pair of blue jeans, held up by pieces of string reaching up over his shoulders. His was now a far different figure from that presented by him in the ring of the Sparling Shows.

After dumping the flour into the cans, in doing which Teddy took his time, he attached a hose pipe to the boiler, under the direction of Henry. Next he filled the cans with water and was then ready to turn on the steam to boil the paste.

Teddy was about to do this when Mr. Snowden appeared on the scene. He looked over the cans critically, but observing nothing that he could find fault with, he got a stick and began poking in the bottom of one of the cans, thinking he had discovered that more flour had been used than was necessary.

All at once Teddy, who was now inside the car, turned a full head of steam through the hose pipe. There being one hundred and forty pounds of steam on the boiler something happened.

The full force of the steam shot into the bottom of the can over which Mr. Snowden was bending. The contents of that can leaped up into the air, water, flour, bluestone and all, and for the next few seconds Manager Snowden was the central figure in the little drama. It rained uncooked paste for nearly half a minute. Such of it as had not smitten him squarely in the face went up in the air and then came down, showering on his head.

The force of the miniature explosion had bowled the manager over. Choking, sputtering, blinded for the moment by the stuff that had got into his eyes, he wallowed in the dust by the side of the car.

Teddy shut off the steam, went out on the platform and sat down.

"What happened?" he demanded innocently. Perhaps he did not know and perhaps he did.

Mr. Snowden did not answer, for the very good reason that he could not. His clothes were ruined.

"It looks like a storm," muttered the lad. In this he was not mistaken.

A happy thought came to him. Springing up he hurried into the car, and, drawing a pail of water from the tap, ran out with it. Mr. Snowden had just scrambled to his feet.

"This will do you good," said Teddy, dashing the pail of water over the manager's head. "That's the way you brought me back when I got pasted up last night."

The Circus Boy ducked back to the platform and sat down to await developments. They were not long in arriving. The instant Snowden got the flour out of his eyes sufficiently to enable him to see he began blinking in all directions.

Finally his eyes rested on Teddy Tucker, who was perched on a brake wheel observing the manager's discomfiture.

"You!" exploded the manager. Grabbing up the paddle used for the purpose of stirring paste he started for the Circus Boy.

Teddy promptly slid from the brake wheel and quickly got to the other side of the car. Snowden was after him with an angry roar, brandishing the paddle above his head.

"I knew it would blow up a storm pretty soon," muttered the lad, making a lively sprint as the manager came rushing around the end of the car. The chase was on, but Teddy Tucker was much more fleet of foot than was his pursuer, besides which his years of training in the circus ring had put him in condition for a long race.

Around and around the car they ran, the porter watching them, big-eyed and apprehensive, but Teddy kept his pursuer at a distance without great effort.

After a short time the lad varied his tactics. Increasing his speed, he leaped to the rear platform of the car, and sprang up on the platform railing. Here, grasping the edge, he pulled himself to the roof, where he sat down with his feet dangling over, grinning defiantly.

"Come down from there!" roared the manager. "I'll teach you to play your miserable pranks on me!" The roof of the car was beyond the ability of Mr. Snowden to reach.

"I'm sorry. I didn't know you had your nose stuck in the paste pot when I turned on the steam," murmured Teddy.

This served only to increase the anger of the man on the ground.

"You did it on purpose; you know you did!" roared Mr. Snowden. "Come down, I tell you."

"You come up. It's fine up here!"

The manager, now angered past all control, uttered a growl. Hastily gathering up a handful of coal he began heaving the pieces at Teddy. But Tucker was prepared for just such an emergency.

>From his pockets he drew several chunks of coal, that he had picked up during his sprinting match around the car. He let these drive at Mr. Snowden, one after the other, not, however, throwing with sufficient force to do much damage. He did not wish to harm his superior, but he did want to drive him off.

Mr. Snowden soon got enough of the bombardment, for he was getting the worst of it all the time.

"I'll turn the hose on you!" he bellowed, making a dash for the interior of the car, where it was his intention to turn on the boiling hot water and steam.

"I guess it's time to leave," decided Teddy. Quickly hopping down he ran and hid behind a freight car a short distance from the show car. When Mr. Snowden came out, grasping the hissing hose, his victim was nowhere to be seen.

Uttering angry imprecations and threats the manager returned to his office, changed his clothes, then strode off up town to a hotel to get a bath, of which he was very much in need at the moment.

"I guess he will be cooled off by the time he gets back," decided Teddy, emerging from his hiding place. "I think I will go back to work. I must earn my money somehow. That man is crazy, but I have an idea he will be sane after I get through with him."

Teddy returned to his paste-making. Henry, the porter, was so frightened that he hardly dared talk to Teddy, for fear the manager might catch him doing so and vent his wrath on the Englishman.

As the Circus Boy had surmised Mr. Snowden returned after a two hours' absence, much chastened in spirit. He did not even look at Teddy Tucker, though the latter was watching the manager out of the corners of his eyes. Mr. Snowden went directly to his stateroom where he locked himself in.

"I guess the storm has blown over," decided young Tucker, grinning to himself. "But won't Phil raise an awful row when he hears about it!"

The lad quickly learned the paste-making trick, and after dinner he set to work in earnest. He found it hard work stirring the stiff paste, and it seemed as if Teddy got the greater part of it over his clothes and face. He was literally smeared with it, great splashes of it disfiguring his face and matting his hair.

When the men from the country routes drove in there was a howl of merriment. The lad did present a ludicrous sight.

"Hello, Spotted Horse!" shouted one of them.

"Hello yourself," growled Teddy, in none too enviable a frame of mind.

"That's the name. That's the name that fits our friend Tucker!" cried Missing Link. From that moment on, aboard Car Three, Teddy Tucker lost his own name and became Spotted Horse.

The men had no sooner unloaded their paste cans than the porter had told them of the trouble that morning between Teddy and the manager.

The men howled in their delight. Mr. Snowden, off in his little office, heard the sounds of merriment and knew that the laughter was at his expense. His face was black and distorted with rage.

"I'll show them they can't trifle with and insult me," he gritted.

At that moment he roared for Billy.

"The regular evening seance is about to begin," announced Billy, with a grimace, as he turned toward the office.

"Bring the cub, Forrest, along!" shouted the manager.

"Who?" called Conley.

"Forrest and that fool friend of his."

"He means Spotted Horse," suggested Rosie. "Run along, Spotted Horse. Got your war paint on?"

"I always have my war paint on," grinned Teddy, as he started toward the private office, following Conley and Phil Forrest.

The three ranged up before the car manager, who surveyed them with glowering face.

"What have you done today?" he demanded, fixing his gaze on Billy.

"We got up more than four hundred sheets of paper."

"Four hundred sheets!" groaned Snowden. "What have you fellows been doing? Sleeping by the roadside?"

"No, sir, we have been working, and Mr. Forrest here pulled off one of the cleverest hits that's ever been made. He plastered a silo that stands out like a sore thumb on the landscape, and which every farmer within ten or twenty miles about will go to look at."

"Humph, I don't believe it! What have the other men done?"

Conley reported as to the number of sheets that the men had posted, whereat the manager rose, pounded his desk and, in a towering rage, expressed his opinion of the tribe of billposters again.

Billy smiled sarcastically, in which he was joined by Teddy, but Phil's face was solemn. He was becoming rather tired of this constant abuse.

"If you have nothing to say to me, I will go back to my place in the car," spoke up Phil.

Snowden glared at him.

"Did I tell you to leave this room?"

"I believe you did not."

"Then stand there until I tell you to go!"

"Very well, sir."

"Conley, I have called you in here to be a witness to what I am about to say. Do you hear?"

Billy nodded.

"During the past two days I have been insulted and abused by those two young cubs there, until it has come to a point where I appear to be no longer manager of this car. Your men outside have laughed at my discomfiture--yes, sir, actually made sport of me."

"I think you are mistaken. I--"

"I am *not*. I am never mistaken. This morning, this fellow Tucker not only defied me, but turned on the steam when I was examining a paste pot, and soaked me from head to foot. Then he ended up by throwing coal at me."

"Yes, and you started the row," retorted Teddy. "The idea of a big man like you pitching on to a boy. You ought to be ashamed of yourself."

"Stop it! I'll forget you are a boy if you goad me further. But I have had enough of it. I'll stand it no longer. Do you understand?"

No one replied to the question.

"This thing has gone far enough. Have you anything to say for yourself or your friend here, Forrest?"

"Yes, sir, I have."

"Say it."

"You are the most ill-tempered man it has ever been my experience to know."

"You're discharged! Both of you! Get off my car instantly! Do you hear me?"

"I could not very well help hearing you. I am sorry to disobey you, but we were ordered to Number Three by Mr. Sparling. We will try to do our duty, but we shall not leave this car until Mr. Sparling orders us to do so," answered Phil steadily.

CHAPTER X
A SURPRISE, INDEED

P hil had triumphed, but he felt little satisfaction in having done so. The manager had ordered the two boys from his office after the interview and the command to leave the car at once. But the lads had stayed on, and had gone about their duties, Phil working with all the force that was in him. He had even stirred Teddy to a realization of his duty and the latter had done very well, indeed.

A week had passed and the car was now in South Dakota. >From there they were to make a detour and drop down into Kansas, whence their course would be laid across the plains and on into the more mountainous country.

Mr. Snowden had studiously avoided the boys; in fact he had not spoken a word to them since the interview in the stateroom, but he had bombarded Mr. James Sparling with messages and demands that the Circus Boys be withdrawn from the car, renewing his threats to leave in case his demand was not complied with.

One bright Sunday morning the car rolled into the station at Aberdeen, South Dakota, and as it came to a stop a messenger boy boarded it with a message for Billy Conley.

Billy looked surprised, and even more so after he had perused the message itself. He quickly left the car, saying he would return after breakfast, but instead of going directly to breakfast, he proceeded to the best hotel in the place, where he called for a certain man, at the desk.

Billy spent some two hours with the man whom he had gone to see, after which he returned to the car. There was a twinkle in his eyes, as he looked at the Circus Boys, who were at that moment getting ready to go to church, a duty that Phil never neglected. He still remembered the time when he used to go to church on Sunday mornings, holding to his mother's hand. Never a Sunday passed that he did not think of it.

"Will you go with us, Billy?" he asked, noting the gaze of the assistant manager fixed upon him.

"Not this morning. I expect company," answered Billy with a grin.

Teddy eyed him suspiciously.

"Billy is up to some tricks this morning. I can see it in his eyes," announced Tucker shrewdly. "I guess I will stay and see what's going on."

"No; you will come with me," replied Phil decisively. So Teddy went.

Shortly after their departure a gentleman boarded the car, at the stateroom end, and walked boldly into the office.

The man was James Sparling, owner of the Sparling Combined Shows.

Mr. Snowden sprang up, surprise written all over his face.

"Why, Mr. Sparling!" he greeted the caller. "I did not expect you."

"No; my visit is something of a surprise, but it is time I came on. Where are the boys?"

"You mean young Forrest and Tucker?" asked the manager, his smile fading.

"Yes."

"The young cubs have gone to church. A likely pair they are! What did you mean by turning loose a bunch like that on me?"

There was a slight tightening of Mr. Sparling's lips.

"What seems to be the trouble with them?"

"Insubordination. They are the worst boys I ever came across in all my experience."

"Have you done as I requested, and helped them to learn the business?"

"I have not!"

"May I inquire why not?"

"My telegrams should be sufficient answer to that question. Both of them are hopeless. I want nothing to do with either of them. They have thoroughly disorganized this car, and each of them has assaulted me. Had I followed the promptings of my own inclinations I should have smashed their heads before this. But I considered their youth."

Mr. Sparling leaned back and laughed.

"I am glad you did not try it."

"Why?" demanded the manager suddenly.

"Because you would have got the thrashing of your life. Mr. Snowden, I am fully informed as to what has been going on in this car."

"So, that's it; those cubs have been spying on me and reporting to you, eh? I might have known it."

"You are mistaken," answered the owner calmly. "While they had sufficient provocation to do so, not a murmur has come from either of them. They have taken their medicine like men. I make it a rule to keep posted on what is going on in every department of my show. I therefore know, better than perhaps you yourself could tell me, what has been going on on Car Three. And it is going to stop right here and now."

"What do you mean?"

"In the first place, the work has been unsatisfactory. The men have done as well as could be expected of them, but they have been in such a constant state of rebellion because of your attitude that the work was bound to suffer."

"You are very frank, sir."

"That's my way of doing business. You not only have neglected the work but you have openly defied me and my orders."

"That's exactly what these young cubs have done with me," interposed the manager quickly.

"My information is quite to the contrary. However, be that as it may, I have decided to make a change."

"Make a change?"

"Yes."

"I do not understand."

"Then I will make it more plain. I'm through with you."

"You mean you discharge me?"

"You have guessed it."

The manager smiled a superior sort of smile.

"You forget I have a contract with you. You can't discharge me until the end of the season."

"And you forget that I have already done so. Here! You see, I come prepared for your objections. Here is a check for your salary to the end of the season. We are quits. I do not have to do even that, but no one can say that James Sparling doesn't do business on the square."

The manager turned a shade paler.

"I--I'm sorry. When--when do you wish me to leave?"

"Now--this minute! I want you to get off this car, and if you don't get off bag and baggage inside of five minutes, I shall make it my personal business to throw you off," announced the showman with rising color. He had contained himself as long as he could. The indignities to which his Circus Boys had been subjected, ever since they joined the car, had stirred the showman profoundly.

"It is now a quarter to twelve. At noon sharp, your baggage and yourself will be outside of this car. I am in charge here now."

The showman leaned back and watched his former car manager hurriedly pack his belongings into a suitcase.

"I'll get even with you for this," snarled Snowden as he walked from the car, slamming the door after him.

"And a good riddance!" muttered the showman rising. "This will be a good time for me to look over the books and find out what shape the car is in."

Mr. Sparling pressed an electric button, and Henry, the porter, responded to the summons.

"Has Mr. Forrest returned yet?"

"No, sir."

"Is Mr. Conley out there?"

"Yes, sir."

"Send him in."

Billy entered the stateroom, a broad smile on his face.

"Sit down, Billy. Well, our friend has gone. I suppose you are sorry?"

"On the contrary," replied Billy promptly, "I am tickled half to death. Now we'll be able to do some real work! We'll show you what we can do! By the way, Mr. Sparling, are you intending to carry out the plan you told me about this morning?"

"Yes. You will have a chance next year."

"Thank you, sir."

"Now, we will go over the books together. I shall have to ask you some questions as we go along. Please first tell the porter to send Phil and Teddy in when they return, but not to tell them who is here."

Billy went out and gave the showman's orders to the porter. As it chanced there were none of the other men of the crew on board the car at that time. They knew nothing about the change that was taking place.

Upon Billy's return he and his chief settled down to a busy few minutes of going over books and reports. The chief found many things that did not please him, and his anger grew apace at some of them.

"I guess I did a good job in getting rid of Snowden. What I should have done was to have got rid of him before I joined him out in the spring."

"He was a bad one," agreed Billy. "I can work with most anybody, but I never could work with the likes of him. The boys are all right. He wouldn't have had any trouble with them if he'd used them like human beings. They both put up with more than I would have stood. But I tell you, that boy, Teddy--Spotted Horse, the boys call him--did hand it out to the Boss. If Snowden had stayed here much longer I'd been willing to lay odds that Teddy would have run him off the car. Did I tell you about how Phil posted the silo?"

"No; what about it?"

Billy began an enthusiastic narration of Phil's clever piece of work, Mr. Sparling nodding as the story proceeded.

"I am not surprised. He is a natural born showman. You will hear great things from Phil Forrest some of these days, and his friend, Teddy, will not be so far behind, either, when once he gets settled down."

"I guess they are coming now," spoke up Conley. "Somebody got on the back platform just now. I'll go out and see."

Billy met the Circus Boys coming in.

"You are wanted in the stateroom," he said.

"More trouble?" laughed Phil.

Billy nodded.

"Maybe, and maybe not, but I reckon the trouble is all over."

Phil and Teddy started for the stateroom. At the door they halted, scarcely able to believe their eyes. There sat Mr. Sparling, smiling a welcome to them.

"*Mr. Sparling!*" cried Phil dashing in, with Teddy close at his heels.

"Yes, I wanted to surprise you," laughed the showman, throwing an arm about each boy.

"I am so glad to see you," cried Phil, hugging his employer delightedly.

"And it does my heart good to set eyes on you two once more. The Sparling organization has not been quite the same since you left. And, Teddy, we haven't had any excitement since you left."

"How's the donkey?"

"Kicking everything out of sight that comes near him. He has not been in the ring since you left," laughed the showman.

"I wish I was back there. I don't like this game for a little bit."

"You mean you do not like the work?"

"Well, no, not exactly that. The work is all right, but--"

"But what?" persisted Mr. Sparling.

"Never mind, Teddy," interposed Phil. "No tales, you know."

"I'm telling no tales. I said I didn't like it and that's the truth. May I go back with you, Mr. Sparling?"

"You may if you wish, of course, if you think you want to leave Phil."

"Is Phil going to stay?"

"Certainly."

Teddy drew a long sigh.

"Then, I guess I'll stay, too, but there's going to be trouble on this car before the season ends, sir."

"Trouble?"

"Yes, sir."

"What kind of trouble?"

"I'm going to thrash a man within an inch of his life one of these fine days."

"I am astonished, Teddy. Who is the man?"

"Oh, no matter. A certain party on this car," replied Teddy airily.

"I sincerely hope you will do nothing of the sort, for conditions have changed somewhat on Number Three. Behave yourself, Teddy, and learn all you can. You may be a car manager yourself one of these times, and all this experience will prove useful to you," advised Mr. Sparling.

"Not the kind of experience I have been having; that won't be useful to me," retorted Teddy.

Mr. Sparling and Phil broke out into a hearty laugh, at which Teddy looked very much grieved.

"Have you seen Mr. Snowden?" questioned Phil, glancing keenly at his employer. There was something about the situation that gave the lad a sudden half-formed idea.

"Yes, I have seen him," answered the showman, his face sobering instantly.

"Where is he?"

"He has gone away. I might as well tell you, boys. Mr. Snowden is no longer manager of this car. He is no longer connected with the Sparling Show in any capacity, nor ever will be again," announced Mr. Sparling decisively.

The Circus Boys gazed at him, scarcely able to believe what they had heard.

"Not--not on this car any more?" questioned Phil.

"Never again, young man."

"Hip, hip, hooray!" shouted Teddy Tucker at the top of his voice, hurling his hat up to the roof of the car, and beginning a miniature war dance about the stateroom, until, for the sake of saving the furniture, Phil grabbed his friend, threw him over on the divan and sat down on him.

"Now, Mr. Sparling, having disposed of Teddy, I should like to hear all about it," laughed Phil.

"He is the same old Teddy. I can imagine what a pleasant time Snowden has had with Tucker on board the same car with him. There is little more to say. I have been disappointed in Snowden for sometime. I had about decided to remove him before you joined the car. I wished, however, to send you boys on, knowing full well that you would soon find out whether there was any mistake in my estimate of the man. Then, too, I had other reasons for sending you in the advance."

"Well, sir, now that he has gone, I will say I am heartily glad of it, though I am sincerely sorry for Mr. Snowden. He knew the work; I wish I were half as familiar with it as he is; but I wouldn't have his disposition--no, not for a million dollars."

"I would," piped Teddy, whom Phil had permitted to get up. "I'd be willing to be a raging lion for a million dollars."

"Have you decided what you are going to do with Car Three now?" inquired

Phil. "You know I am interested now that I have cast my lot with it."

"Yes; I certainly have decided. Of course the car will go on just the same."

"I understand that, but have you made up your mind who you will appoint as the agent--who will be manager of the car?"

"I have."

"I presume we shall have to get a man before we can go on?"

"Yes."

"Then we shall have to lie here a day, at least. Well, we can busy ourselves. We are slighting a good many of these bigger towns. They are not half-billed."

"I am glad to hear you say that. It shows that you are already a good publicity man. But you will not have to lie here any longer than you wish," added the showman significantly.

"Will you tell me who the new manager is, Mr. Sparling?"

"Yes. You are the manager of Car Three!" was the surprising reply.

CHAPTER XI
THREE CHEERS AND A TIGER

M an--Manager of Car Three?" stammered Phil.

"Yes."

Teddy's eyes grew large.

"*That*--manager of Car Three?" he said derisively.

Mr. Sparling gave him a stern glance.

"But, Mr. Sparling, I know so little about the work. Of course I am proud and happy to be promoted to so responsible a position, but almost, if not every man on the car, is better equipped for this work than I am."

"They may be more familiar with some of the details, but as a whole I do not agree with your view. In two weeks' time you will have grasped the details, and I will wager that there will not be a better agent in the United States."

The Circus Boy flushed happily.

"You will have to be alive. But I do not need to say that. You always are alive. You will have to fight the railroads constantly, to get your car through on time; you will have to combat innumerable elements that as yet you have not had experience with. However, I have no fear. I know the stuff you are made of. I ought to. I have known you for nearly five years."

"I will do my best, Mr. Sparling."

There was no laughter in the eyes of the Circus Boy now.

"Then again, you are going right into territory where you will have the stiffest kind of opposition. At least five shows are booked for our territory almost from now on."

"Have any of them billed that territory?"

"I think the Wild West Show has. The others are about due there now."

"It is going to be a hand-to-hand conflict, then?"

"Something of that sort," smiled the showman. "I shall expect you to beat them all out."

"You are giving me a big contract."

"I am well aware of that. We all have to do the impossible in the show business. That is a part of the game, and the man who is not equal to it is not a showman."

Phil squared his shoulders a little.

"Then I will be a showman," he said, in a quiet tone.

"That is the talk. That sounds like Phil Forrest. It is usual for shows to have a general agent who has charge of all the advance work, and who directs the cars and the men from some central point. Heretofore I have done all of this myself, but our show is getting so large, and there is so much opposition in the field, that I have been thinking of putting on a general agent next season. However, we will talk that over later."

"And so you are the car manager, eh," quizzed Teddy.

"It seems so."

"Won't I have a snap now?" chuckled the lad.

"Yes; your work will be done with a snap or back you go to Mr. Sparling, young man," laughed Phil. "There will be no drones in this hive."

"What have you been doing?" inquired the owner.

"I'm the dough boy."

"The dough boy?"

"He has been making paste," Phil informed him.

Mr. Sparling laughed heartily.

"I guess we shall have to graduate you from the paste pot and give you a diploma. I cannot afford to pay a man seventy-five dollars a week to mix up flour and water."

"And steam," corrected the irrepressible Teddy.

"Should not some press work be done from this car?" asked Phil.

"By all means. It is of vast importance. Hasn't it been done?"

"No, sir; not since I have been on board. I would suggest that we turn Teddy loose on that; let him call on the newspapers, together with such other work as I may lay out for him. Teddy is a good mixer and he will make friends of the newspaper men easily."

"A most excellent idea. I leave these matters all in your hands. As to matters of detail, in regard to the outside work, I would suggest that you consult Conley freely. He is a good, honest fellow, and had he a better education he would advance rapidly. I intend to promote him next season. Conley told me, this morning, of your brilliant exploit in billing the silo."

"Oh, you saw him this morning? Now I understand why he hurried away and came back all smiles. You--you told him I was to be manager?"

"Yes."

"What did he say?"

"He was as pleased as a child with a new toy. He said you were a winner in the advance game."

"Will he tell the men?"

"No. That will be left for you to do in your own way."

Phil nodded reflectively.

"And now let us go into the details. We will first look over the railroad con-tracts, together with the livery, hotel and other contracts. I am going to leave you five hundred dollars in cash, and each week you will send in your payroll to the treasurer, who will forward the money by express to cover it. The five hundred is for current expenses. Spend money with a lavish hand, where necessary to advance the interests of the show, and pinch every penny like a miser where it is not neces-sary. That is the way to run a show."

Phil never forgot the advice.

"And Teddy?"

"Yes, sir."

"You may, in addition to your other duties, act as a sort of office assistant and secretary to Phil. I shall make only one request of you. Write to me every night, giving a full account of the day's doings, with any suggestions or questions that Phil may ask you to make, and enclose this with the report sheet. You understand, Phil, that your regular detailed reports go to the car behind you. The one that comes to me is a brief summary."

"I understand."

"Have you the route?"

"No, sir."

"Perhaps it is in the desk. Yes; here it is. Now and then we shall have to make changes in it, of which I shall advise you, in most instances, by telegraph. Wire me every morning as to your whereabouts so I may keep in touch with you."

"You may depend upon me, sir."

"I know it."

For the next half hour Mr. Sparling and Phil were deeply engaged in poring over the books, the contracts and the innumerable details appertaining to the work of an advance car.

"There, I guess we have touched upon most everything. Of course emergencies will arise daily. Were it not for those anyone could run a car. No two days are alike in any department of the circus business. You will meet all emergencies and cope with them nobly. Of that I am confident. And now, Mr. Philip Forrest, I officially turn over to you Advertising Car Number Three of the Sparling Shows. I wish you good luck and no railroad wrecks. Come and have lunch with me; then I'll be getting back to the show. The rest is up to you."

"Mr. Sparling," said Phil with a slight quaver in his voice, "if I succeed it will be because of the training you have given me. I won't say I thank you, for I do not know whether I do or not. I may make an awful mess of it. In that case I shall suffer a sad fall in your estimation. But it is not my intention to make a mess of it, just the same."

"You won't. Come along, Teddy. We will have a meal, and it won't be at a contract hotel, either," said the showman, with a twinkle in his eyes.

The three left the car. Several of the men had returned from their lunch, and the word quickly spread through the car that Mr. Sparling was there. Rumors of high words between the showman and Snowden were rife, but none appeared to know anything definite as to what had really occurred.

Conley knew, but he preserved a discreet silence.

"I reckon, if they wanted us to know what was going on they would tell us," declared Rosie the Pig. "That's the trouble with these cars. We ain't human. We ain't supposed to know anything."

"Rosie, don't talk. Someday you might make a mistake and really say something worth listening to," advised Slivers.

For some reason the men evinced no inclination to leave the car. They hung about, perhaps waiting for something to turn up. Each felt that there was something in the air, nor were they mistaken.

It was nearly three o'clock when Phil and Teddy returned to the car. Mr. Sparling was not with them. The lads went direct to the office, unlocked the door and entered.

The men looked at each other and nodded as if to say, "I told you so," but none ventured to speak.

After what seemed a long wait Phil stepped from the office, followed by Teddy. They heard the lads coming down the corridor. Phil stopped when he reached the main part of the car. His face was solemn.

"Boys," he began, "I have some news for you. Mr. Sparling has been here today, as you probably know."

Some of the men nodded.

"The next piece of news is that Mr. Snowden has closed with the car. He is no longer manager."

Phil paused, as if to accentuate his words. The men set up a great shout. It was a full minute before they settled down to listen to his further remarks.

"What I am about to say further is the most difficult thing I ever did in my life. I would prefer to turn, or to try to turn, a triple somersault off a springboard. Mr. Sparling has appointed me manager of Car Three. I suppose, instead of Phil Forrest, I shall be referred to as The Boss after this."

The whole crew sprang to their feet.

"Three cheers for The Boss!" shouted the Missing Link.

"Hip, hip, hooray! Tiger!" howled the crew, while Phil stood blushing like a girl. Teddy was swelling with pride.

"I'm it, too," he chimed in, tapping his chest significantly.

"Boys," continued Phil, "I probably know less about the actual work of the advance than any man here. Anyone of you can give me points."

"No, we can't," interrupted several voices at once.

"I am also younger than any of you. I know a great deal about the business back with the show, but not much of what should be done ahead. But I am going to know all about it in a very short time. While I shall be the Boss, I am going to be the friend of every man here. You are not going to be abused. Just so long as you do your work you will be all right. The first man caught shirking his work closes then and there. But I shall have to look to you for my own success. I'll work **with** you. I understand that we have strong opposition ahead of us. Let's you and me take off our coats, tighten our belts, sail in with our feet, our hands and our heads--and beat the enemy to a standstill! Will you do it?"

"We will, you bet!" shouted the crew.

"We will beat them to a frazzle," added Rosie the Pig.

"That will be about all from you, Rosie," rebuked the Missing Link.

"This car leaves at eight o'clock this evening. After we get started, come in and I will give you all your assignments for tomorrow. My friend, Teddy, has been promoted to the position of press agent with the car, and a few other things at the same time. Henry, you will attend to the paste-making, beginning tomorrow. This being a billboard town, I am going to skip it and get into the territory where the opposition is stronger. I have arranged with the local billposters to take care of the work here."

"That is all I have to say just now, boys. When you have anything to ask or to suggest, you know where the office is. Mr. Conley, will you please come to the office now? We have quite a lot to talk over."

The men gave three rousing cheers.

Phil Forrest had made his debut as a car manager in a most auspicious manner, at the same time winning the loyalty of every man on the car.

CHAPTER XII
FACING AN EMERGENCY

Well, this is what I call pretty soft," chuckled Teddy Tucker. Car Three was under motion again, bowling along for the next stand, fifty miles away. The lads were sitting in their cosy office, Teddy lounging back on the divan, Phil in an easy chair at the roll-top desk. The lights shed a soft glow over the room; the bell rope above their heads swayed, tapping its rings with the regularity of the tick of a watch.

"Who sleeps upstairs, you or I?" asked Teddy.

"I will, if you prefer the lower berth."

"I do. It has springs under it."

"You will wish it had no springs, one of these nights, when you get bounced out of bed to the floor. Do you know that Pullman cars have no springs?"

"No; is that so?"

"That is the fact."

"Why?"

"Because, on rough or crooked roads, most of the passengers would be sleeping in the aisle. All hands would be bounced out. You are welcome to the lower berth."

"Shall we turn in and try them?"

"No; I am going to wait until we get to our destination. I want to see that the car is properly placed, in view of the fact that this is our first night in charge. I want to know how everything is handled by the railroad. You may go to bed if you wish."

"No; I guess I will sit up. I have a book to read. This is too fine to spoil by going to bed. I could sit up all night looking at the place. Why, this is just like being on a private car, isn't it?"

"It is a private car."

There were delays along the route to the next stand, and the car was laid over for more than an hour at a junction point, so that it was well past midnight when they reached their destination.

Phil and Teddy both went outside when the train entered the yards, Tucker hopping off as they swung into the station.

"Where are you going?" called Phil.

"Going to see if I can find anything that looks like food," answered Teddy, strolling away. "My stomach must have attention. It's been hours since it had any material to work with. Will you come along?"

"No; I am going to bed as soon as we get placed."

"Bad habit to go to bed on an empty stomach," called back the irrepressible Teddy.

The train that had drawn them uncoupled and started away; in a few moments a switching engine backed down, hooked to the show car and tore back and forth through the yards, finally placing the car at the far side of the yard behind a long row of freight cars.

All the men on board were asleep, and now that the car would not be disturbed before morning, Phil entered his stateroom and went to bed.

He had not been asleep long when he felt himself being violently shaken. A hand, an insistent hand, was on his shoulder.

"Phil, wake up! Wake up!"

The boy was out of bed instantly.

"What is it? Oh, that you, Teddy? What did you wake me up for?"

"You'll be glad I did wake you when you hear what I have to say."

"Then hurry up and say it. I am so sleepy I can scarcely keep my eyes open. What time is it?"

"Half-past one."

"Goodness, and we have to get up before five o'clock! What is it you wanted to tell me? Nothing is wrong, I hope."

"I don't know. But there is something doing."

"Well, well, what is it?"

"I think there is another show car in the yards."

"A show car?"

"Yes."

"You don't say!"

"I **do** say."

"Who's car is it?"

"I didn't wait to look. I saw the engine shift it in."

"Where is it?"

"Way over the other side of the station, on the last track."

Phil sprang for his trousers, getting into them in short order, while Teddy looked on inquiringly.

"Anybody would think you were a fireman the way you tear into those pants. What's your rush?"

"Rush? Teddy Tucker, we have business on hand."

"Business?"

"Yes, business. It's mighty lucky for us that your appetite called you out. I shall never go to sleep again without knowing who is in the yard, and where. Come and show me where they are."

"I'm sorry I told you."

"And I am mighty thankful. You see, something told me to leave that last town and hurry on."

"Something tells me to go to bed," growled Teddy.

"You come along with me, and be quiet. Was the car dark?"

"I guess so."

The boys hurried from Car Three; that is, Phil did, Teddy lagging behind.

"Over that way," he directed.

Phil crawled under a freight car to take a short cut, and ran lightly across the railroad yards. The boys passed the station; then, crossing several switches, they beheld a big, yellow car looming up faintly under the lights of the station.

"It is an advertising car," breathed Phil. "I wonder whose it can be?"

"You can search me," grumbled Teddy. "Guess I'll go back to bed now."

"You wait until I tell you to go back," commanded Phil. "Keep quiet, now."

The Circus Boy crept up to the car with great caution. The light was so faint, however, that he was obliged to go close to it before he could read the letters on the side of it. Even then he had to take the letters one by one and follow along until he had read the length of the line.

"Barnum and Bailey's Greatest Show on Earth," was what Phil Forrest read, and on the end of the car a big figure "4."

"Car Four," he muttered. "Here's trouble right from the start. I am right in the thick of it from the word go."

Phil walked back to where Teddy was awaiting him.

"Find out whose car it is?"

"Yes; Barnum & Bailey."

"Humph! Let's go back to bed."

"There will be no bed for us tonight, I fear. Wait; let me think."

Phil walked over and sat down on a truck on the station platform, where he pondered deeply and rapidly.

"All right; I have it figured out. We have our work cut out for us. You wait here while I run back to the car."

Teddy curled up on the truck, promptly going to sleep, while Phil hurried to the car to get the address of the liveryman who had the contract for running the country routes for the show.

The lad came running back, and, darting into the station, found a telephone. After some delay he succeeded in reaching the livery stable.

"This is Car Three of the Sparling Shows," he said. "Yes, Car Three. I want those teams at our car at two o'clock this morning. Not a minute later. Can't do it? You've got to do it! Do you hear what I say? I want those teams there at two o'clock. Very well; see that you *do!*"

Out to the platform darted Phil in search of Teddy. The latter was snoring industriously.

Phil grabbed him by the collar and slammed him down on the platform.

"Ouch!" howled Teddy.

"Get up, you sleepy-head!"

"I'll friz you for that!" declared Tucker, squaring off pugnaciously.

"Don't be silly, Teddy. This is the first emergency we have had to face. Don't let's act like a couple of children. We must beat the opposition, and I'm going to beat them out, no matter what the cost or the effort. Listen! I want you to go to the contract livery stable. Here is the address. Go as fast as your legs will carry you."

"What, at this time of night?"

"Yes."

"Not I!"

"You go, or you close right here, young man. Come now, Teddy, old chap, re-member the responsibility of this car rests on your shoulders almost as much as on mine. Let's not have any hanging back on your part."

"I'm not hanging back. What is it you want me to do? I'm ready for anything."

"That's the talk. Hustle to the livery stable and camp right on the trail. See that those teams are here at two o'clock, or by a quarter after two, at the latest. Have the men drive up quietly, and you show them the way. Don't you go to sleep at the stable. Now, foot it!"

Teddy was off at a dogtrot. His pride was aroused.

"I guess we'll clean 'em up!" he growled as he hurried along.

In the meantime, Phil hastened into the station and ran to the lunch room. It was closed.

"Pshaw!" he muttered.

Phil now turned toward town on a brisk run. After searching about, he found an all-night eating place that looked as if it might be clean.

"Put me up ten breakfasts. I have some men that I want to give an early start. They haven't time to come here. Wrap up the best breakfasts you can get together. Put in a jug of coffee and a jug of milk. I will call for the food inside of half an hour. Don't delay a minute longer than that. Hustle it!"

Phil darted out and back to the car. Every nerve in his body was centered on the work in hand. He ran to Conley's berth and shook him.

"What is it?" mumbled Billy sleepily.

"Get up and come into the stateroom. There is business on hand."

Billy hopped out of bed, wide awake instantly, and ran to the stateroom.

Phil briefly explained the situation and what he had planned to do. After he had finished Billy eyed him approvingly.

"You're a wonder," he said. "What about breakfast?"

"I am having some prepared at a restaurant. But the men will not have time to eat it. They may take it with them and eat it on the road."

"I'll rout out the crew," returned Billy, hurrying back into the car.

There was much grumbling and grunting, but as soon as the men were thoroughly awake they were enthusiastic. Not a man of them but that wanted to see this bright-faced, clean-cut young car manager beat out his adversaries.

By the time the men had washed and dressed the rigs began to arrive. These were quickly loaded with brushes, paste cans and paper, all with scarcely a sound, the men speaking in subdued tones by Phil's direction.

The darkness before the dawn was over everything.

At last all was in readiness.

Phil handed each man his route.

"Now, boys, it is up to you. I look to you to put the Greatest out of business, for one day at least. You should be out of town and on the first daub inside of thirty minutes. I will go with you and pick up the breakfasts; then you will go it alone. Don't leave a piece of board as big as a postage stamp uncovered. Wherever you strike a farmer, make him sign a brief agreement not to let anyone cover our paper. Pay him something in addition to the tickets you give him. Here is an agreement that you can copy from. Make your route as quickly as you can and do it well; then hurry back here. I may need you."

"Hooray!" muttered Rosie the Pig.

"Hold your tongue!" commanded Billy, "Think this is a Fourth of July celebration?"

"Go ahead!"

Phil hopped into one of the wagons, and off they started. It was but the work of a few minutes to load the packages of breakfast into the wagons, after which the men drove quickly away. Phil paid the bill. But he was not yet through with his early morning work. He made his way to the livery stable.

"Send another rig over to the car at once. I want you to bring the day's work of lithographs and banners here, and my men will work them out from your stables. I do not want the opposition car to know what we are doing until it is nearly all done."

"Whew, but you're a whirlwind!" grinned the livery stable man.

The horse and wagon were made ready at once, Phil riding back to the car with it. The banner-men and lithographers who were to work in town had not been awakened. Phil wished them to get all the sleep possible; so, with Teddy's help, he loaded the paper on the wagon and sent the driver away with it. Then he awakened the rest of the men.

Phil briefly explained what had happened.

"Now, I want all hands to turn out at once. Go to the restaurant on the third street above here and get your breakfasts. Here is the money. By daylight some of the business places will begin to open. I want every man of you to spend the fore-noon squaring every place in town. Make an agreement that no other show is to be allowed to place a bill in their windows. While you are eating your breakfasts I will lay out the streets and assign you. I have the principal part of the town in my mind, now, so I can give you the most of your routes. Teddy, you will turn in and help square. I will collect the addresses of the places you have squared, early in the morning, and by that time I shall have a squad of town fellows hired, to place the stuff. Now, get going!"

All hands hurried into their clothes; after locking the car, Phil led them to the restaurant. But the Circus Boy did not take the time to eat. Instead he busied him-self laying out the routes for the town men to work.

By the time that they had finished their breakfast faint streaks of dawn were appearing in the east.

"Now, boys, do your prettiest!" urged Phil.

"We will; don't you worry, Boss."

The men hurried off, full of enthusiasm for the work before them, while Phil started out to round up a squad of men to distribute the lithographs after his own men had squared the places to put them.

In an hour he had all the men he wanted. This done, Phil took his way slowly back to the railroad yards and stepped up to the platform of his own car. The freight cars had been removed from in front of him and the rival car stood out gaudily in the morning light. All was quiet in the camp of the rival. Not a man of its crew was awake.

"I hope they sleep all day," muttered Phil, entering his own car and pulling all the shades down, after which he took his position at a window and watched from behind a shade.

CHAPTER XIII
A BAFFLED CAR MANAGER

It was nearly seven in the morning when Phil's vigil was rewarded by the sight of a man in his pajamas, emerging from the rival car. The man stood on the rear platform and stretched himself. All at once he caught sight of Car Three. The fellow instantly became very wide awake. Opening the car door he called to someone within; then three or four men came out and stared at the Sparling car.

"They are pretty good sleepers over there, I guess," grinned the rival car manager, for such he proved to be.

The men dodged back, and there was a lively scene in the rival car. The men realized that they had been remiss in their duty in sleeping so late, but still they had not the least doubt of their ability to outwit their rivals, for the crew of Car Four was a picked lot who had never yet been beaten in the publicity game.

About this time Phil Forrest strolled out to the rear platform of his car. He was fully dressed save for coat and vest and hat, yet to all appearances he, too, had just risen.

The manager of the rival car came out and hailed him.

"Hello, young fellow!" he called.

"Good morning," answered Phil sweetly.

"Seems to me you sleep late over there."

"So do you," laughed Phil. "There must be something in the air up this way to induce sleep."

"I guess that's right. Who are you?" inquired the rival manager.

"I am one of the crowd."

"You're the programmer, perhaps?"

"I may be most anything."

The manager of the rival car strolled toward Car Three, whereupon Phil started, meeting him half-way. For reasons of his own he did not wish his rival to get too close to the Sparling car.

"I never saw you before," said the rival, eyeing Phil keenly.

"Nor I you."

"What's your name?"

"Philip."

"Glad to know you, Philip. How long have you been with the car?"

"A few weeks only."

"Who's your car manager?"

"A fellow named Forrest."

"Never heard of him. Is he in bed!"

"No; he is out."

"Humph! What time do you start your men on the country routes?"

"Usually about seven to seven-thirty."

"Well, you won't start them this morning at that time."

"No; I think not."

"I'll tell you what you do; you come and take breakfast with me. We won't go to any contract hotel, either."

"Thank you; I shall be delighted. Wait till I get my clothes on."

Phil hastened back to his own car.

"That fellow is playing a sharp trick. He is trying to get me away so he can get his men out ahead of mine. I will walk into his trap. He knows I am the manager. I could see that by the way he acted."

Phil stepped out and joined his rival.

"I believe you said you were the manager of that car, did you not?" asked the rival.

"I am, though I do not recollect having said so."

"A kid like you manager of a car? I don't know what the show business is coming to, with all due respect to you, young man."

"Oh, that's all right," answered the Circus Boy with a frank, innocent smile. "I am just learning the business, you know."

"I thought so," nodded the rival. "My name's Tripp--Bob Tripp."

"You been in the business long?"

"Fifteen years, my boy. After you have been in it as long as I have, you will know every crook and turn, every trick in the whole show business," said the fellow proudly. "You are a bright-faced young chap. I should like to have you on my car. Don't want a job, do you?"

"No, thank you. I am very well satisfied where I am. I can learn on a Sparling car as well as anywhere else, you know."

"Yes, of course."

The couple stopped at the leading hotel of the town, where the rival manager ordered a fine breakfast. Phil Forrest was quite ready for it. He already had done a heavy day's work and he was genuinely hungry.

"Guess they don't feed you very well with your outfit," smiled Tripp.

"Contract hotels, you know," laughed Phil. "I do not get a chance at a meal like this every day."

"Do the way I do."

"How is that?"

"Feed at the good places and charge it up in your expense account."

"Oh, I couldn't do that. It would not be right."

"That shows you are new in the business. Get all you can and keep all you get. That's my way of doing things. I was just like you when I began."

They tarried unusually long over the meal, Tripp seeming to be in no hurry. Phil was sure that he was in no hurry, either. And he knew why there was no need for hurry. Bob, in the meantime, was relating to the show boy his exploits as a manager. In fact he was giving Phil more information about the work of his own car than he realized at the time.

Now and then the Circus Boy would slip in an innocent question, which Bob would answer promptly. By the time the meal was finished Phil had a pretty clear idea of the workings of his rival's advance business, as well as their plans for the future, so far as Tripp knew them.

"By the way, how did you happen to get a berth like this, young man?" questioned Tripp. "I thought a fellow by the name of Snowden was running Car Three for old man Sparling."

"He was."

"Closed?"

"Yes."

"What for?"

"I would rather not talk about that. You will have to ask headquarters, or Snowden himself. You see, it is not my business, and I make it a rule never to discuss another fellow's affairs in public."

"Nor your own, eh?"

"Oh, I don't know. I think I have talked a good deal this morning. But you and I had better get back to our cars and get our men started, had we not? This is a late morning all around."

"No hurry, no hurry," urged Bob. "Why the men haven't got back from their breakfast yet. Wait awhile. Have a smoke."

"Thank you; I do not smoke."

Tripp looked at him in amazement.

"And you in the show business?"

"Is that any reason why a man's habits should not be regular?"

"N-n-n-o," admitted the rival slowly.

"Well, I must be going, just the same. I have considerable work to do in the car."

Bob rose reluctantly and followed Phil from the dining room. He had hoped to detain the young car manager longer, or until his own men could get a good start on the work of the day.

He looked for no difficulty, however, in outwitting his young opponent.

As they approached the railroad yards each car stood as they had left it, shades pulled well down and no signs of life aboard.

"Looks as if your crew was still asleep," smiled Tripp.

"I might say the same of yours, did I not know to the contrary," answered Phil suggestively.

Bob shot a keen glance at him.

"What do you mean?"

"Nothing much. Of course I did not think your men would be asleep all this time. They are surely out to breakfast by this time."

"You ain't half as big a fool as you look, are you?" demanded the rival manager.

"Well, I will see you later."

Each went to his little office and began the work of the day, but there was a grim smile of satisfaction on the face of each.

Fully an hour passed, and one of the lithographers from the rival car went aboard with the information that they were unable to get a piece of paper in any window in town thus far.

"Why not?" demanded Tripp.

"They say their windows are already contracted for," was the answer.

"Contracted for?"

"Yes."

"By whom?"

"I don't know. That's all the information we can get."

"Seen any other showmen about town this morning?"

"No; not any that I know, nor any with paper and brush under his arm."

"H-m-m-m," mused the showman. "That's queer. It can't be that the young man across the way has got the start of us. No; that is not possible. He is too green for that. Have his men gone out on the country routes yet, or are they still asleep?"

"I don't know. Nobody has seen a living soul around that car this morning, so far as I know."

"I'll go over town and do a little squaring on my own hook. I'll soon find out who has been heading us off, if anyone has."

The manager hurried off with his assistant, but even he was unable to get any information.

He was baffled and perplexed. He did not understand it. Tactics entirely new had been sprung on him. He was an expert in the old methods of the game, but these were different.

In the meantime, Phil Forrest, the young advance agent, sat calmly in his state-room, now and then receiving a report from Teddy Tucker who sauntered in under cover of a string of freight cars on the opposite side, then slipped out again.

Teddy was Phil's blockade runner this day.

At noon the party on the rival car all adjourned for luncheon, and there they were joined by their manager, who discussed the queer situation with them. This was the time for Phil Forrest.

"Now for the surprise," he said, hurriedly going uptown, where he got his own lithographers together, and the crew that he had hired in town. Every man had been pledged to silence, as had the livery stable man and his helpers.

"Now, shoot the stuff out! Get every window full before those fellows are through their dinner. A five-dollar bill for the man who covers his route first. The banner locations we cannot fill so quickly, but they are all secured, so our friend can't take them away from us. Now get busy!"

They did. The men of Car Three forgot that they were hungry. Never before had the lithographers and banner men worked as they did that day. With the extra help that Phil had put on he was able to cover the ground with wonderful quickness.

When the men of the rival crew emerged from the contract hotel, and sat down in front to digest the contract meal, they suddenly opened their eyes in amazement.

In every window within sight of them there hung a gaudy Sparling circus bill, some windows being plastered full of them.

They called the manager hastily.

"Look!" said his assistant.

"What! We're tricked! But they haven't got far with their work. They haven't had time. Don't you see, the lazy fellows have just got to work. After them, men! Beat them out! You've got to out bill this town!"

As the men hurried out into the other streets the same unpleasant sight met their eyes. Every available window bore a Sparling bill; every wall obtainable had a Sparling banner tacked to it. One could not look in any direction without his gaze resting on a Sparling advertisement.

Bob Tripp was mad all through.

He had been outwitted.

In his anger he started for Car Three. Reaching it he discovered the young advance agent on the shady side of Car Three, lounging in a rocking chair reading a book.

Phil's idea of dramatic situations was an excellent one.

"What do you mean, playing such a trick on me?" demanded the irate rival.

The Circus Boy looked up with an innocent expression on his face.

"Why, Mr. Tripp, what is it?"

"Is that the way you repay my hospitality?" he shouted.

"Please explain."

Phil's tone was mild and soothing.

"You have grabbed every hit in this town. It's unprofessional. It's a crooked piece of business. I'll get even with you for that."

"Why, Mr. Tripp, how can that be, I am green; I am only a beginner, you know," answered the Circus Boy, with his most winning smile.

Bop Tripp gazed at him a moment, then with an angry exclamation turned on his heel and strode back to his own car.

Half an hour later Phil Forrest's men drove in from their country routes. They had covered them quickly, having got such an early start.

Phil heard their reports. They had left nothing undone. Phil then hurried over town to pay the bills he had contracted, first leaving word that not a man was to leave the car until his return.

He was back in a short time.

"We go out at two o'clock, boys," he announced upon his return. "I am leaving the banner men here. They will take a late train out tonight, and join us in the morning."

An express train came thundering in, and before Bob Tripp knew what was in the wind it had coupled on to Car Three. A few moments later Phil Forrest and his crew were bowling away for the next stand. His rivals would not be able to get another train out until very late that night.

Late in the afternoon Bob Tripp's country crew returned, tired, disgusted and glum.

"Well, what is it?" demanded the now thoroughly irritated manager.

"Not a dozen sheets of paper put up by the whole crew," was the startling announcement. "That Sparling outfit has plastered every spot as big as your hand for forty miles around here."

"What! Why didn't you cover them?" shrieked the manager.

"Cover them--nothing! They had every location cinched and nailed down. Every farmer stood over the other fellow's paper with a shot gun."

"Sold! And by a kid at that!" groaned Bob Tripp settling down despairingly into his office chair.

CHAPTER XIV
TEDDY WRITES A LETTER

I'm only a beginner," mused Phil Forrest, as his car spun along at a sixty-mile gait. "And I'm green, and I have a whole lot to learn, but if Bob Tripp catches up with Car Three, now, he will have to travel some!"

The next town was made quite early in the afternoon. Phil, however, did not settle down to wait for another day. He had wired the liveryman in the next town to meet his car, so, immediately upon arrival, he bundled his billposters off on the country routes.

"Work as far as you can before dark, then find places to sleep at a farmhouse. Do the best you can. We must be out of these yards before noon tomorrow, and as much earlier as possible. If you can post by moonlight do it, even if you have to wake the farmers up along the line to get permission."

The men were well-nigh exhausted, but they rose manfully to the occasion. They realized that there was a master hand over them, even if it were the hand of a boy inexperienced in their line of work.

No manager had ever reeled off work at such a dizzy pace as Phil Forrest was doing. It challenged their admiration and made them forget their weariness.

The country routes started, Phil set his lithographers at work. The men kept at it until nearly midnight. They had completed their work in the town and in the meantime Phil and Teddy had squared the hits, as they are called--the places where the banners were to be tacked up--all ready for the banner men to get to work when they arrived in town next morning, or late that night.

They arrived about midnight, but the other car did not come on the train with them. They brought the information that the train was a limited one, and would not carry the rival car. Bob Tripp would not be able to get through until sometime the next forenoon.

Phil felt like throwing up his hat and shouting with delight, but his dignity as a car manager would not permit him to do so. No such limitations were imposed upon Teddy Tucker, however, and Teddy whooped it up for all that was in him.

All hands were weary when they turned in that night. At about eleven o'clock the following morning, the country billposters came in, having completed their routes. Phil had made his arrangements to have his car hauled over the road by a special engine, and shortly after noon Car Three was again on its way, every man on board rejoicing over the drubbing they had given their rival.

Phil Forrest was a hero in their eyes. Not a man of that crew, now, but who would go through fire for him, if need be!

That afternoon the same plan was followed, Phil driving his men out to their work.

"I am sorry, boys," he said. "I don't like to drive you like this, but we've simply got to shake off Tripp and his crew. In a day or so we will be straightened around again so we can settle down to our regular routine, unless, perhaps, we run into more trouble. You have all done nobly. If it hadn't been for you I should have been whipped to a standstill by that other outfit."

"Not you," growled the Missing Link. "They don't grow the kind that can whip the likes of you," in which sentiment the entire crew concurred.

No more was seen of Bob Tripp and his men on that run. Tripp heard from his general agent, however, with a call-down that made his head ache. The general agent kept the telegraph wires hot for twenty-four hours, and in the end, sent another car ahead of Tripp into the territory that Phil Forrest and his men were working.

Phil, of course, was not aware of this at the time, but he found it out before long.

His car had slipped over into Kansas, by this time, and the crew were now working their way over the prairies.

"It seems to me that it is time you were attending to your press work, Teddy Tucker," said Phil on the following day. "You have not called at a newspaper office since we started under the new arrangement."

"Nope," admitted Teddy.

"Why not?"

"Why, do you think?"

"I am sure I do not know."

"Well, you ought to, seeing you have been keeping me running my legs off twenty-four and a half hours out of every day."

"You have been pretty busy, that is a fact. But you had better start in today. You have plenty of time this afternoon to attend to that work."

"What shall I tell them?"

"Oh, tell them a funny story. Make them laugh, and they will do the rest."

"But I don't know any funny stories."

"Tell them the story of your life as a circus boy. That will be funny enough to make a hyena laugh."

"Ho, ho!" exploded Teddy. "It is a joke. He who laughs first laughs last."

"You mean 'he who laughs last laughs best,'" corrected Phil, smiling broadly.

"Well, maybe. Something of the sort," grinned the Circus Boy.

"And look here, Teddy!"

"Yes?"

"Have you written to Mr. Sparling yet, as he requested you to do?"

"No."

"And why not?"

"Same reason."

"You must write to him every day, no matter how busy you are. Sit up a little later every night; go without a meal if necessary, but follow his directions implicitly."

"Implicitly," mocked Teddy.

However, Mr. Sparling was not without news of what had been going on on Car Three. Billy Conley had written fully of Phil Forrest's brilliant exploits. After one of these letters, Mr. Sparling wrote Conley, as follows:

"Those boys will never tell me when they do anything worthwhile. It isn't like Phil to talk about his own achievements. So you write me anything of this sort you think I would like to know. I do not mean you are to act as a spy, or anything of the sort. Just write me the things you think they will not write about."

Bill understood and faithfully followed out his employer's directions. Mr.

Sparling proudly showed Conley's letters to all of his associates back with the show, where there was much rejoicing, for everyone liked Phil; not only liked but held him in sincere admiration for his many good qualities.

That evening, however, Teddy sat down at the typewriter and laboriously hammered out a letter to his employer.

"Hang the thing!" he growled. "I wish I had only one finger."

"Why? That's a funny wish," laughed Phil. "Why do you wish that?"

"Because all the rest of them get in the way when I try to run a typewriter."

"I am afraid you never would make a piano player, Teddy."

"I don't want to be one. I would rather ride the educated donkey. It's better exercise." Teddy then proceeded with his letter. This is what he wrote:

"Dear Mr. Sparling:"

"Nothing has happened since you were here."

One of the lithographers had a fit in the dining room of the contract hotel this morning (I don't blame him, do you?) and they hauled him out by the feet. We run amuck with another advance car, the other day, but nobody got into a fight. I thought rival cars always--excuse the typewriter, it doesn't know any better-- got into a fight when they met.

"One of the billposters fell off a barn--it was a hay barn, I think. I am not sure. I'll ask Phil before I finish this letter. Let me see, what happened to him? Oh, yes, I remember. He broke his arm off and we left him in a hospital back at Aberdeen. Phil let one of the banner men go this morning. The fellow had false teeth and couldn't hold tacks in his mouth. I tell him it would be a good plan to examine the teeth of all these banner men fellows before he joins them out, just the same as you would when you're buying a horse. Don't you think so?"

"By the way, I almost forgot to tell you. We ran over a switchman in the night last night. I don't think it hurt the car any."

"Well, good-bye. I'll write again when there is some news. How's January? Wish I was back, riding him in the ring. Expect I'll have an awful time with him when I start in again. Don't feed him any oats, and keep him off the fresh grass. I don't want him to get a fat stomach, because I can't get my legs under him to hold on when he bucks."

"Well, good-bye again. Love to all the boys."

"Your friend,"

"Teddy Tucker."

"P. S. Did I tell you we killed the switchman? Well, we did. He's dead. He's switched off for keeps."

"T. T."

"P. S. Yes, Phil says it was a hay barn that the billposter fell off from. Wouldn't it be a good plan to furnish those fellows with nets? Billposters are scarce and we can't afford to lose any good ones."

"T. T."

CHAPTER XV
IN AN EXCITING RACE

More trouble," announced Teddy, one morning a few days later, when the boys awoke in Lawrence, Kansas.

"What's the trouble now, Old Calamity?" demanded Phil, who was washing his face and hands.

Contrary to his usual practice, he had not looked from his stateroom window immediately upon getting up. Teddy had, however. His eyes grew a little larger as he did so, but otherwise the sight that met them did not disturb his equanimity in the least.

"The usual."

"What do you mean? Have we run over another man?"

"Worse than that."

"You are getting to be a regular calamity howler."

"I'm a showman, I am. I keep my eyes open and I know what's going on about me. That's more than you can say for some people not more than a million miles away."

"All right; I will take that for granted. But tell me what it is that is disturbing you so early in the morning?" questioned Phil with a short laugh.

"We're all surrounded," answered Teddy grimly.

"Surrounded?"

"Yes."

"I don't understand."

"You will, pretty soon."

"Surrounded by what?"

"Opposition."

"What!"

"What's the matter, can't you hear this morning?"

"I hear very well, but I don't understand what you mean when you say we are surrounded by opposition. It strikes me we have been surrounded by nothing else since we took charge of Car Three."

Teddy nodded.

"Yep, that's right. But this is different. On our left, if you will observe closely, you will notice the canary yellow of Car Three of the so-called Greatest Show on Earth. On your right, if you still keep your eyes open and look hard, you will discover the flaming red of the Wallace advance car. And--"

"What!"

"And, as I was saying, if that fails to make an impression on you, a glance to the rear will discover to your feeble eyesight, one John Robinson's publicity car."

Having delivered himself of this monologue, Teddy calmly sat down and began to draw on his trousers, yawning broadly as he did so.

"Methinks, milord, that trouble is brewing in bucketfuls," he added.

Phil sprang to the car window, threw up the shade and peered out. He stepped to the other side of the car, looking from the window there.

"You're right."

"Of course I am right. I'm always right. How does it happen you did not discover all this after we got in last night!"

"They were not here then. They must have come in afterwards."

Dashing out into the main part of the car Phil called the men.

"Wake up, fellows!"

"What's up," called a voice.

"The yards are full of opposition. Three advertising cars are here besides our own."

No other urging was necessary to get the crew out of bed. They came tumbling from their upper berths like as many firemen upon a sudden alarm. All hands ran to the windows and peered out.

"Sure enough, they are all here," shouted Conley. "I reckon they have caught us napping this time."

"No; they are not awake yet. I hope they sleep as well as Bob Tripp's crew did," answered Phil. "But we have a big job before us today. You had better hustle through your breakfasts, boys. I will call up the livery and get the country routes off at once. Perhaps we can get ahead of the other fellows."

Phil did so, but as his teams drove up another set swung over the tracks, pulling up before the canary car.

"Hustle it! Hustle it!" cried Phil. "You drivers, if you get out ahead of the others and keep ahead, you'll get a bonus when you come in tonight."

Each side was now striving to get away first. The crew from the canary car made the getaway ahead of Phil's men, but they had less than a minute's headway.

The Circus Boys had their coats off and were hustling cans of paste over the side of the car into the wagons. Every move on their part counted. There was not a particle of lost motion.

Phil sprang into the first wagon to leave.

"Come on, fellows! Never mind the horses. I can buy more, if these break their necks."

With a rattle and a bang both rigs smashed over the tracks, and were on their way down the village street, each team on a runaway gallop. Phil's team was gaining gradually.

"Hang on to the cans!" shouted the Circus Boy. "We are coming to a bad crosswalk!"

People paused on the street, not understanding what the mad pace meant. A policeman ran out and raised his stick. Teddy, who had hopped on behind at the last minute, not wishing to lose any of the fun, now stood up unsteadily, hanging to the driver's coat collar and nearly pulling that worthy from his seat.

They overhauled the first wagon from the canary car and passed it.

"Ye--ow!" howled Teddy as their wagon swept by. "This is a Wild West outfit!"

The paste cans in the two wagons were dancing a jig by this time. Teddy suddenly lost his grip on the driver's collar, sitting down heavily on the nearest can. At that moment they struck the rough crossing, whereat Teddy shot up into the air, landing in a heap by the side of the road.

"Whoa!" commanded Phil, at the same time jumping on the can to keep it from following in the wake of Teddy.

"Go on!" howled Teddy, partially righting himself.

The driver urged his horses on and the team sprang away with loud snorts. But the rival wagon had taken a fresh start, and was drawing up on the Sparling outfit, the rear team, with lowered heads, appearing to be running away.

These horses struck the crosswalk with a mighty crash. The rear wheels slewed. The big can of paste was catapulted over a fence, narrowly missing Teddy Tucker's head as it shot over him. He flattened himself on the ground, but was up like a flash, sprinting out of harm's way.

There was reason for his last action. Other things were coming his way. As the wheels of the rival wagon slewed, they struck a gutter.

The wagon turned turtle, and men, paste brushes, paper and all were scattered all over the place.

"Oh, that's too bad!" muttered Phil. "But we can do nothing for them if we stop. There are plenty back there to lend assistance."

His tender heart told him to go back, whether he could be of service to his rival or not, but his duty lay plain before him. He must outdistance the enemy.

A second team came plunging down the road from the canary car, close behind the unfortunate wagon. These horses, too, were instantly mixed in the wreck. The wagon did not turn turtle as the one before it had done, but one of the horses went down.

Now came other wagons of the Sparling outfit. They were running two abreast in the road. But the drivers saw the obstruction in time, slowed down and dodged it. They were off at a tremendous speed, and a few moments later branched off on different roads, quickly disappearing in a cloud of dust.

Phil's wagon crew discovered a farm barn just ahead of them. They drove up to it on a run. All hands piled out. And how they did work! In a few moments the old barn was a blaze of color.

"First blood for the Sparling Combined Shows!" shouted the boy. "Now hit the trail for all you are worth!"

They were off again. A cloud of dust to their rear told them that one of their rival's wagons was after them. At the next stop the pursuing wagon rolled by them, the men yelling derisively.

"It is the Wallace Show's crowd!" shouted Phil. "Get after them."

The Wallace people went on half a mile further. As Phil drew up on them he shouted to his driver to go on to the next stop. When they made it finally, they were passed by the crew from the canary advance car.

It was give and take. Such billing never had been seen along the Kansas highway before. But, up to the present moment, the Sparling crew had much the best of it.

"This won't do, boys; I have got to get back. I have no business here. Keep this right up. Don't lag for an instant. Is there a town near here?"

The driver informed Phil that there was one about a mile ahead of them.

Phil rode on until he reached it. Here he jumped out, taking a bundle of paper with him, ordering his men to drive on. With him he carried a bucket of paste and a brush.

Phil went to work like a seasoned billposter, plastering every old stable and tight board fence in the village. By the time the rival crews drove in there was little space left for them, and such spots as were left were all on back or side streets.

"I guess they will know we have been here," decided Phil. "Now I must find a way to get back to the car."

Inquiring at the post office he learned where he might be able to hire a rig.

Losing not a minute the boy hunted up the man who owned the horse, and, by offering to pay him about twice what the service was worth, got the fellow to take him back.

The journey back to town was executed in almost as good time as that which Phil had made in driving out. The rig rattled into town at a gallop, and Phil was landed on his car again, safe and sound after his exciting rides.

"Did you beat them," cried Teddy, as Phil drove up.

"We did and we didn't. But we have got the start of them on the billing. Were any of the other men hurt?"

"One of the canary bird crowd got a broken arm. The others were pretty well bruised up, but they are still in the ring."

"What is doing in the town?"

"I sent our men out to square the locations. Told them not to put up any paper, but to hustle the squaring."

"Good for you, Teddy! You are a winner. Where did you learn that trick?"

"Oh, it's a little trick I picked up the other day. I'm a professional publicity man, you know."

"Are our opposition friends doing the same thing?"

"I think not. I got the start of them by fully an hour. Worked the same game on them that we did on Tripp the other day. You remember?"

Phil nodded. Indeed, he did remember.

"The men were so excited over the race that they couldn't spend time to attend to business. I got a pretty good bump, but I thought it was a good time to get back in the town and hustle our fellows, seeing that you had hit the long trail. I didn't expect you back before the middle of next week, the rate you were going."

Phil laughed good-naturedly.

"You remain here and watch the car, Teddy. I am going to run over town. Had your breakfast?"

"Say, I forgot all about that. I haven't had a thing."

"Your appetite will keep. I must look around a little. Something may be going on that needs attention from our side."

Phil had reason, a few minutes later, to be thankful that his instinct had prompted him to hurry over town.

CHAPTER XVI
A BATTLE OF WITS

The Robinson people, at least, have got to work," muttered the Circus Boy as he made his way downtown. Here and there, at rare intervals, he came across a window bill of the show mentioned.

There were blocks of windows, however, with no billing in them. Phil interpreted this to mean that his own men had secured the requisite permission to place their own bills there.

He smiled as he thought of the little trick. It was an idea of his own to square locations ahead of the lithographers. Ordinarily, the lithographer made his rounds with a bundle of bills on his arm. Entering a store he would say, "May I place this bill in your window?" Phil had adopted the plan of sending the men around first. After they had obtained the signed permission they would go back over the same ground and place the bills. This took a little more time, but it had the merit of fooling his rivals and getting many more places squared than could have been done in the old way.

Suddenly a great wall loomed ahead of him.

Phil paused and surveyed it critically.

"Wouldn't I like to fasten Sparling banners all over that place, though. What a hit that would be. Why," he added looking about him, "it could be seen pretty much all over town."

Phil started on, intending to find out who owned the building. As he did so he saw a man from the canary-colored car entering the building. The man was going into a store on the ground floor.

"I'll bet he is after that very wall. Oh, pshaw! Why didn't I stay in town and attend to my business, as I should have done, instead of racing over the country at that mad pace? I'm going over to see what he is up to."

The Circus Boy hurried along. Entering the store he saw the man from the rival car, who proved to be the manager of it, engaged in earnest conversation with a man whom Phil supposed to be the proprietor.

After a little the manager of the other car hurried out. Phil stepped forward.

"Are you the proprietor?" he asked politely.

"Yes; what can I do for you?"

"Do you own this building?"

"No, but I am the agent for it."

"Very good. You are the man I want to talk with. I am from the Sparling Shows. I should like the privilege of fastening some banners on that south wall there."

"You're too late, young man. I just gave the other man permission to do that."

"Did he pay you?" asked Phil sweetly.

"No."

"Did you sign a contract with him?"

"No."

"May I ask how much he is to give you for the privilege?"

"Twenty-five dollars."

"He ought to be ashamed to offer you such a mean figure as that for such a privilege."

The proprietor grew interested.

"Where has he gone?"

"Said he had to talk with someone back with the show by long distance telephone before he could close the bargain."

Phil glanced apprehensively at the door.

"I guess you had better sell the privilege to me while you have the chance. He may not come back, you know; then you will be out all around."

"I couldn't think of it. I gave him the privilege of buying the wall."

"Money talks, doesn't it, sir?"

"It does, young man. It always makes such a loud noise around me that I can't hear much of anything else."

Phil grinned.

"Yes; it's pretty noisy stuff."

The lad calmly drew a big roll of bills from his pocket, placing it on the counter before the storekeeper. To the pile he added his watch, a jackknife, a bunch of keys and a silver matchbox.

"Help yourself," he begged calmly.

"Wha--what?" gasped the storekeeper.

"I said help yourself. I want that wall. I leave it to you to say what is a reasonable price for it--a price fair to you and to me. You admit that money talks. This money is addressing its remarks to you direct, at this very moment."

The proprietor hesitated, glanced at the money and other articles that Phil had arrayed so temptingly before him, and turned reflectively facing the rear of the store.

"I will scribble off a little contract," said Phil softly. "How much shall we make the consideration?"

"What'll you give?"

"I've got him!" was Phil Forrest's triumphant thought, but he allowed none of his triumphant feeling to appear in his face.

"Well, were I making the offer I should say the wall was worth about forty dollars, no other bills to appear on it until after my show has left town. But I told you to help yourself. I'll stick to my word."

"Count me out forty dollars and take it. I like your style. Your way of doing business makes a hit with me."

Phil inserted the agreed-upon price in the contract.

"Just sign your name there, please," he said, still in that soft, persuasive voice.

The storekeeper read the brief contract through, nodded approvingly, then affixed his signature with the fountain pen that Phil had handed to him.

This done, the lad counted out forty dollars, stowed the rest away in his pockets, together with his other belongings, then extended his hand cordially to the proprietor.

"Thank you very much," murmured Phil, his face all aglow now.

"You're welcome. When do you put up your bills?"

"At once. We leave town tonight, and we have a lot of work to do first."

"Let's see; were you one of the fellows mixed up in that race this morning?"

Phil blushed.

"I am afraid I was very much mixed up in it. Well, good afternoon."

The lad turned and started for the door. At that moment someone entered. It was the manager of the canary car.

"It's all right. I'll take the location," he announced, smiling broadly, as he walked rapidly to where the proprietor was standing, laying two tens and a five-dollar bill on the counter.

"I--I'm sorry," stammered the storekeeper, flushing. "I have just sold it to another party."

"Sold it!"

The manager's face went several shades paler.

"Yes."

"To--to whom?"

"To that young gentleman there."

The manager whirled and faced Phil.

"Who--who are you?"

"My name is Forrest," answered Phil, smiling easily. He could well afford to smile.

"And you--you have bought this location?"

"I have."

"Whom do you represent?"

"The Sparling Combined Shows."

The Circus Boy's rival flushed angrily.

"I demand that the location be turned over to me instantly! It belongs to me, and I'll have it if I have to fight for it. Here's my money, Mr. Storekeeper. I command you to make out a paper giving me the right to bill that wall."

"I do not think he will do anything of the sort, my dear sir," spoke up Phil. "I have bought and paid for the location and I propose to hold it. You had no more right to it than any other man. You did not have the nerve to put down your money for it when you had the chance, and you lost your opportunity. You will see the wall covered with Sparling banners in a very short time."

"I will not!"

"Be on your way, my man. Let me tell you the Sparling banners are going up."

"There's my money!" shouted the manager of the canary colored car. "The wall is *mine!*"

He dashed out of the store and started for his car on the run.

"If you let those other showmen banner the wall I'll have the law on you!" announced Phil sternly. Then the Circus Boy ran out of the store, starting off at a lively sprint for his own car. He caught up with the rival manager in a moment, passed him and bounded on. His rival already was puffing and perspiring under the unusual effort.

"Turn out every man in town!" he called, dashing into the car. "Teddy, run to the main street and send everyone of our banner men and lithographers to the Ward Building. You and Henry carry over there at once all the banners you can scrape together. Do not lose a minute. But wait! I'll telephone the liveryman for a wagon to carry the paper, brushes and paste pots over. You remain here, Henry, and go with the wagon. Teddy, you hustle for the men. Run as if the Rhino from the Sparling menagerie were charging you!"

Teddy leaped from the car platform and was off, with Phil sprinting after him in long strides.

They passed the manager of the canary colored car just as they were running across the switches in the railroad yard. He was only then getting to his car.

CHAPTER XVII
THE CHARGE OF THE PASTE BRIGADE

Phil's plans were formed instantly.

He ran to a place where he had seen a painter's sign earlier in the day. Reaching there he ordered the painter to send out to the Ward Building a gang of painters with their swinging platform, tackle and full equipment, telling the man briefly what was wanted of him after the apparatus reached the building in question.

"Now hurry it, and I'll double the price you ask if you get there and do the work I am asking of you."

The painter needed no further inducement. Once again money made its announcement in unmistakable tones.

Phil again started off on a run. Reaching the Ward Building he found his banner men and lithographers gathering. A few moments after his arrival the livery wagon with the paste, brushes and paper, came dashing up with Henry, the porter, standing guard over it. Teddy had thoughtfully turned out all the available men in the livery stable and came charging down the street, driving them before him, howling at every jump. That is, Teddy was howling; as he did whenever the occasion presented itself.

By this time quite a crowd had been attracted to the scene, not understanding what all the excitement was about. None of the rival posters had appeared as yet. Phil had got a very good start.

Telling off three of his banner men he sent them to the roof, while the painter was preparing to swing his scaffold.

"I am afraid I shall have to block your store for a short time, Mr. Storekeeper," said Phil, entering the store. "Our friend is going to try to take the place by storm,

I think, and we shall have to stand him off."

"He had better not try it," growled the proprietor.

"He will, just the same. But, with your permission, he will not get upstairs to the roof while I am here."

"Do whatever you like. I've got his money, but it's here for him when he wants it."

Phil, having arranged with the proprietor, went out and gave his final instructions to his men.

"You are not to let a man through here unless with my permission," he said. "I am going up to the roof. If anything occurs, call me at once. Teddy, I leave the front of the store in your hands while I am away. There is trouble brewing. I feel it in my bones."

"Yes; trouble for the other fellow," grinned Teddy.

In a very short time the painters had succeeded in swinging their scaffold over the roof. An interested crowd was watching the proceeding from the street.

The banner men climbed down on the swinging platform, and, as if by magic, the Sparling banners began appearing on the big wall.

About this time shouting down in the street drew the attention of Phil Forrest. Stepping to the edge of the roof he looked down. A crowd was pressing his men back.

In the lead was the manager of the canary car.

"Drive them off!" roared Phil. "Don't let them get by you!"

"We will!" shrieked Teddy Tucker, now in his element.

Phil turned and hurried down the ladder to the upper floor, then took the stairs in a series of jumps until he had reached the ground floor.

Teddy Tucker had proved himself a real general. He had armed his forces with paste brushes, which he had first thoroughly soaked in the sticky paste pots.

Teddy was dancing up and down the line.

"Paste them, fellows!" he roared. "Paste them good and proper. We'll stick them to the walls when we get them properly daubed!"

With a yell the Sparling crowd began wielding the paste brushes. They wielded them effectively, too. Every sweep of the brushes found a human mark.

Shouts of rage followed the onslaught, above which could be heard the voice of the manager of the canary car, urging the crowd on to violence.

Phil came dashing out.

"Drive them back!" he shouted. "But be careful that you do not hurt anybody. Keep your heads, men!"

"Look out--the police are coming!" shouted a voice.

"Never mind the police! Give it to them!" cried the rival.

A squad of bluecoats came charging down the street.

"Steady, fellows! Don't do anything that will cause the police to take you in," cautioned Phil.

The crowd in front gave way as the police charged in; and, as they did so, the Circus Boy pushed his way to the front of his own line.

A sergeant made for him with upraised club, but Phil did not flinch.

"Wait a minute, officer!" he cautioned.

"I arrest you for disturbing the peace!" was the stern reply.

"You will do nothing of the sort, sir. We have not broken the peace. We are within our rights, protecting our own property and the property of this gentleman," pointing to the proprietor of the store.

"Arrest them! They are stealing my property!" came the cry from the rival manager.

"I guess you had better both come over to the police station, and we will let the captain settle this," decided the sergeant.

"Wait!" commanded the rival. "I have here an injunction commanding this fellow to stop work. I have bought the right to banner this location, and he has stepped in and taken it away from me."

"Is this right?" demanded the sergeant, appealing to the storekeeper, whom he knew well.

"No, it's all wrong. That man has bought nothing. He left his money on my counter after I had sold my wall to this young man here."

"Is this right?" repeated the sergeant turning to Phil.

"I am inclined to think it is. If that man has obtained an injunction, he has done so by false representation. Here is my contract, properly signed, giving us the right to put up our banners, and that is exactly what we are going to do in spite of all the police in the state. You can't stop us. You had better not try."

The sergeant glanced over the paper and scratched his head. He was at a loss what to do. At that moment a lieutenant came running up, demanding to know what the trouble was about.

The sergeant explained, handing the contract to his superior. After perusing it, the lieutenant passed the paper back to Phil.

"You can't stop this man as long as he is not disturbing the peace. That fellow's injunction is not worth the paper it is written on. This is a contract as plain as the nose on your face."

"That is the way it strikes me," answered Phil, with a pleasant smile.

"Disperse the crowd. Keep half a dozen men on duty here, and, if there is any further disturbance, lock them all up."

"Thank you," said Phil, edging near the lieutenant. "And, now that the matter is all settled, if you will call at the Sparling advance car this afternoon, at five o'clock, I shall be happy to furnish you with tickets for yourself and family. That is not a bribe, because we have got the matter all straightened out."

The lieutenant smiled.

"I'll do it," he said. "Five o'clock, you say?"

"Yes."

"Now, get out of here, the whole crowd of you. And you, young fellow," indicating the manager of the canary rival, "if you create any further disturbance in this town, you'll go to the cooler, and stay there. Do you understand?"

The rival manager tried to protest, but the lieutenant started for him.

"I want my money!" he shouted.

"Come and get it. I don't want your money."

"I told you that before," called the storekeeper.

"Go, get your money, and get out of here!" commanded the lieutenant.

Crestfallen and now thoroughly subdued, the manager of the canary car made his way through the crowd; his money was thrust into his hands; then, calling upon his men to follow him, he hurried away.

"There, I guess we won't hear any more from our canary bird friend today," decided Teddy, strutting about and throwing out his chest.

"Not today, perhaps," answered Phil Forrest; "but I am thinking we have not heard the last of him yet. We shall have to look pretty sharply, or he will get the best of us yet. This is a game that one person cannot expect to win at every day. Boys, you may go back to your lithographing now. The police will see that we are protected until we have finished bannering this building."

Phil walked off half a block to survey the work going on high up in the air.

"That location is worth five hundred dollars to any show," he mused. "And I got it for forty. Good job!"

CHAPTER XVIII
THE MISSING SHOW CARS

The work was completed late that afternoon. The Sparling crowd had got the best of their rivals in the window work as well. Sparling show bills were everywhere.

But Phil was thoughtful. He did not like the methods he was obliged to follow, yet he knew that it was a part of the show business. He had the satisfaction, too, of knowing that he had done nothing unfair. He had got the best of his rivals by perfectly fair methods, and he would pursue no others, no matter how badly he was beaten.

After making a round of the town, during which he had twice passed the scowling manager of the canary car, Phil returned to his own car, as there were frequently matters arising there that needed his attention. He found a telegram awaiting him from Mr. Sparling.

"The greatest work ever done by an advance car. I congratulate you all. Keep it up," was what Phil read.

Phil rubbed his forehead in perplexity.

"Now, how in the world did he find out about this so soon, I wonder?" questioned the boy. As a matter of fact, the manager of the Robinson Show's car, who was a friend of Mr. Sparling, had wired him of the day's doings. It was too good to keep, and then again Mr. Sparling's friend was too delighted at the downfall of Snowden, the man whom he thoroughly disliked, to be at all jealous of Phil's triumph.

Phil went over to the yardmaster to find out what train he would be able to go out on that night.

"We are going to send the whole bunch of you out on number 42," was the reply.

"What time does number 42 leave?"

"Half-past eleven."

"What do you mean by 'the bunch of us'?"

"All you advance car fellows. I have got to do that. That is the only train through tonight. You will have to go on that or wait until tomorrow morning."

"Very well; I do not know as I care whether my rivals go on the same train or not. It would do me no good if I did object."

That night the unusual sight of four advance cars hooked together was presented to those who chanced to be in the railroad yards when number 42 pulled out of the station.

Car Three had been coupled up first, the others being hooked on behind it, with the canary car at the rear.

"I am afraid we shall not cut a very big slice tomorrow, Teddy," said Phil after they had got under way.

"Why not?"

"What, with all those crews working against us? It will be a case of three to one. Of course we shall do as much as any one of them, and perhaps a little more, but we cannot expect any great results."

"Maybe I can think of something," mused Teddy.

"I wish you might."

"What would you say to ditching the other fellows?" asked Teddy innocently.

"Teddy Tucker, I am ashamed of you!" exclaimed Phil.

"Sometimes I am ashamed of myself, I am so easy. If it wasn't for my tender heart, Phil, I would have been a great showman by this time."

"Yes, it really is too bad about your tender heart. I--"

His words were cut short by a jolt that nearly threw the lads from their chairs.

"Collision!" yelled Teddy. "Brace yourself!"

"Don't get excited," laughed Phil. "They have forgotten or neglected to couple the airbrake pipes up. Someday one of these crews will wreck us all. I have talked until I am tired. You see there is air on the front end of this train, but these show cars have not been coupled up with the air pipes of the regular train. It is very bad business. I'll report it when we get in tomorrow."

"Let me. I know how to do it up brown."

"No, I will attend to it myself."

"Say, Phil!"

"Yes?"

"If the air was coupled on and the train broke in two in the middle what would happen?"

"Why it would bring everything up standing. Breaking the air circuit would set the brakes the entire length of the train."

"And if the air was not coupled up, what then?"

"In that event nothing would happen."

"The train wouldn't stop?"

"No."

"H-m-m."

"Why do you ask?"

"For information. What do you suppose I am asking for unless I want to know."

Teddy relapsed into a moody silence.

"Why don't you go to bed?" Teddy asked after awhile, looking up suddenly.

"I guess it would be a good idea," replied Phil. "We shall have to get up rather early in the morning. I will set my alarm for three o'clock. I have an idea some of the rival crews will be up and out about that time. They won't be so easily beaten tomorrow."

"Oh, I don't know," answered Teddy. "Maybe so and maybe not. You can't most always sometimes tell."

"Aren't you going to turn in?" demanded Phil, beginning to undress.

"No, not yet. I am not very sleepy tonight."

"You will be, in the morning, and you will not want to get up," cautioned Phil.

"I will take the chance."

Teddy picked up a book and settled himself to read.

Little conversation passed between them after that, and Phil, tumbling into his berth, was soon asleep.

Teddy eyed him narrowly. He waited until his companion was sleeping soundly; then Teddy got up and strolled out to the rear platform. It was deserted. The trainmen did not come back that far, because the doors of the show cars were kept locked so they could not. Show people do not like strangers about them.

Teddy lay down on the platform, peering down between the cars.

"No, no air is coupled on. They ought to be ashamed of themselves," he muttered. "I guess they must have fixed it up for me on purpose."

Teddy opened the door of Car Three softly, listened, then closed it again. Next he leaned out and looked along the tracks, which he could see fairly well, for the moon was now shining brightly.

"I guess there is no grade here." Stepping across to the platform of the car to the rear of him, the boy partially set the brake until he could feel it grinding on the wheels.

"Now, I think we are all ready," he muttered, as, stepping back to the platform of his own car, he grasped the coupling lever firmly with both hands, giving it a mighty tug.

At first it would not budge. The drawheads of the couplers of the two cars were straining because of the drag of the brake that he had but just set.

Teddy loosened the brake a little, then tried the coupling lever again.

This time it swung over with a bang. The lad lost his balance for an instant, and nearly went overboard.

"My, that was a close shave," he exclaimed, hanging desperately to the platform railing, the wind blowing about him in a perfect gale.

"Hello, I wonder what has become of our friends?" laughed the Circus Boy to himself.

Teddy had uncoupled Car Three from the others in their rear, and the cars of his rivals were dropping behind rapidly. He could see the dim lights in the car nearest to him, but even these were rapidly disappearing. A few minutes later as the train swept around a bend, the rival advertising cars disappeared from sight. Teddy knew that they would stop in a few minutes, and lie there stalled.

Teddy Tucker had done a very serious thing, but in his zeal he thought he had accomplished a great feat. Well satisfied with his efforts the lad entered his own car softly, undressed in the corridor and crept quietly to bed. In a very short time he was snoring, sleeping the sleep of peace and innocence.

Teddy hardly moved again that night, until he was roused out by Phil at three o'clock the next morning.

The lad grumbled sleepily and finally tumbled out rubbing his eyes.

Phil stepped out to the rear platform before dressing, for a breath of the fresh morning air.

"Why, Teddy!" he called through the open door.

"What?"

"The opposition cars are not here. The other train must have carried them on. I wonder if those fellows are stealing a march on us?"

"Is that so?"

"Yes; come out and see for yourself."

Teddy stumbled out to the platform, gazed about sleepily and looked solemn.

"No, not here," he said, turning back into the car.

Phil was worried. He could not imagine exactly what the plans of his rivals might be.

"I will wire on to the next stand as soon as the telegraph office opens, and find out if they are there," he decided.

In the meantime Teddy was taking his time about dressing, while the men of the crew were hurrying into their clothes. Phil did the same, then dropped from the car and walked about the yards, rather expecting to find the cars of his rivals hidden behind freight cars.

They were nowhere in sight.

"Well, it cannot be helped, even if we are beaten into the next stand. This is a small place, but an important one. I cannot afford to skip it, no matter if the other fellows have."

Teddy went about his morning duties as usual, solemn faced and silent, but there was a triumphant gleam in his eyes that Phil Forrest as yet had failed to observe.

Phil was pacing up and down on the platform station, waiting uneasily for the operator to appear. After making ready, the men went off to breakfast, Teddy hanging about the car, busying himself with trifling matters. The car seemed to hold an unusual interest for him that morning.

At six o'clock the livery rigs drove up and the rural route men were soon off for their day's work. Phil started the lithographers and banner men out soon thereafter.

About that time the operator arrived; Phil wrote a message to the liveryman at the next town, inquiring if his rivals had reached there.

The answer came back that nothing had been seen of them. They had not even passed through. The operator at the other end said they were at Salina, where Phil's car was at that moment.

This was a puzzler.

"I am afraid it will take a better railroad man than I am to figure this problem out," mused Phil. "Hey, Teddy!"

"Yep?"

"What do you suppose could have become of those other cars?"

"How should I know?"

"They were on this train last night, when we started, and they have not arrived at the next stand yet. They surely are not here."

"Maybe they got a hot journal and had to stop," suggested Teddy.

"Nonsense! Something has happened to them. However, it is not my business to worry about my rivals. As long as I know they are not ahead of me I shall not disturb myself. It is up to me to improve the opportunity and bill this town from one end to the other," decided Phil, starting off over town.

The work went on at a lively pace, Phil urging his men to greater efforts, momentarily expecting to see the canary and red cars come rolling into town.

But no cars came. The next train from the direction Phil had come was not due until nearly noon, the road being a branch road with little traffic over it.

After a time Phil strolled down to the railroad station.

"Any news?" he asked.

"Yes," answered the operator. "They have found the cars."

"Where?"

"It seems they broke away from the train during the night and lay on the main track until morning. One of the crew walked back ten miles to the next station to ask for an engine to pull them out. They will be here on the next train."

"Funny the train crew did not discover that when they put us on the siding here. I do not quite understand it yet?" Phil walked slowly back to his own car, thinking deeply.

CHAPTER XIX
PHIL'S DARING PLAN

Teddy was sitting on the platform of Car Three narrowly watching Phil as he approached.

"Anything doing?" he asked.

"Yes."

"What is it--have you heard from the opposition?"

"Yes. It seems their cars broke away from us during the night, and lay all night on the main track miles from anywhere."

"You don't say!" exclaimed Teddy, in well feigned surprise.

"That is what happened. We are in luck this morning, Teddy Tucker. I suppose I should be sorry for our rivals. But it is the chance of war. We all have to take them in the show business."

"We do," answered Teddy sagely. "At least the other fellow does. When are they coming in?"

"About noon, I understand. I should think someone would lose his job for that piece of carelessness. If it were my car that had been laid out there would be trouble; I can assure you of that."

"Yes; I wouldn't stand for a mean trick like that myself."

Phil stroked his chin and surveyed Teddy thoughtfully. Light was beginning to dawn upon him. All at once he recalled his companion's questions about the air brake pipes the night before.

He fixed his gaze upon Teddy Tucker's scowling face.

"Young man, do you know anything about those cars breaking away?" demanded Phil sternly.

"I understand they broke away--don't you know that the train broke in two?"

"Yes," answered Phil dryly; "I have heard something to that effect."

Phil stepped over to examine the coupling of his own car, Teddy watching him furtively.

"What I want to know is how it happened," continued Phil.

"Why don't you ask the train crew? They ought to know."

"I'll ask you instead. You uncoupled those cars, didn't you?"

Teddy nodded slowly, his eyes on the ground.

"Is it possible that you did a thing like that?"

Teddy nodded again, demanding sullenly:

"Well, we beat 'em, didn't we?"

"Yes; but do you know what would happen, were it known what you have done?"

"I'm easy. What would happen?" Teddy was rapidly assuming a belligerent attitude.

"You would be arrested, and nothing could keep you from state's prison, Teddy Tucker."

"Oh, fudge!"

"You may scoff all you will. It is the truth, nevertheless. I should not be surprised if there were an investigation over this affair--"

"And you'll go tell all you know, won't you?"

"Not unless I am put under oath. If I am, and am asked, I shall have to tell the truth. I ought to sail in and give you a good thrashing here and now."

"You can't do it!"

"Perhaps not, but I could try." A smile struggled to dissipate the clouds on Phil's face. "Listen to me! Do you know that you might have imperilled a great many lives by that foolish act of yours"

"No. How?"

"In the first place, being cut loose from our train as they were, they might have continued on, provided we were on a down or up grade and--"

"We weren't. I looked to see," interjected Teddy.

"Oh, then you admit the charge. I am glad that you have confessed."

"I haven't confessed!" shouted Teddy, his face growing very red.

"If you said that on trial it would be jail for you for some years to come. To return to the subject under discussion, all the men were asleep in those cars, or at least they were supposed to be. Had there been another train over the road, last night, the chances are that it would have run into those show cars and killed every man in them, besides wrecking the train itself and killing a lot more people. I am willing to take long chances in the line of duty, but I should hope I never would commit a crime in so doing. Let this be a warning to you, Teddy Tucker. Never do a thing like this again. We will beat our rivals by all fair means and we will stop there."

Phil paused, eyeing his companion sternly.

Teddy glanced up inquiringly.

"Is the sermon over?" he asked.

"I have no more advice to offer at the present moment. I hope for your sake that the inquiry in this matter will not extend to us. If it does, I feel sorry for you."

An inquiry did follow. It was stirred up most thoroughly by the manager of the canary colored car. But, fortunately for Teddy Tucker, no suspicion of the truth ever dawned upon the rival manager, and the railroad got out of the scrape by disciplining the train crew that had lost the three cars without knowing it. However, the lesson was a wholesome one for Teddy, even though he would not admit the fact. The lesson lasted him pretty nearly all the rest of the season.

The three rival cars came rolling into the yards early in the afternoon of that day. All hands were angry and ready for trouble. Phil passed the time of day pleasantly with his opponent of the previous day, but the manager of the yellow car did not deign to make any reply to his greeting.

The hour was late before he was able to start his men out, and by that time Phil's crew had pretty well covered the town and the surrounding country, though the posters of the latter territory had very long drives, and were not expected to return until very long after dark.

Phil chafed under this, fearing that he would be obliged to miss the last train out that night, which would again put him on the same train with his rivals next day.

One of his men would have a thirty-five-mile drive back after he had finished his day's work. That would bring the man "home," as the return to the car is called, long after midnight in all probability.

Inquiry at the station and a wire to the division superintendent failed to get a special engine to haul Car Three out that night. But in his talk with the station agent Phil learned something that set him thinking. He pondered over the information he had obtained, for sometime.

"I believe I can do it," he muttered. "Talk about Teddy taking long chances, I am going to try to take some chances tonight that are far more dangerous. But I must do something."

Phil had seen a section gang go out in the morning. They had not come in yet, so the Circus Boy strolled over toward the station shortly after six o'clock waiting for the section gang to return.

They did not come in until after seven o'clock.

As the men were going by the station, having put their handcar away, Phil motioned to the foreman of the gang, a bright faced Irishman.

"How are you?" greeted Phil smilingly.

The foreman waved a hand, at which Phil beckoned the man to come to him.

"Are there any more trains over this division tonight?"

"Only number forty-two going west."

"She is due shortly after midnight, is she not?"

"Yes."

"Do you like to go to the circus, Pat?"

"I do."

"Have you a family?"

"I have."

"Will you do me a favor if I give you tickets to the show for yourself and family?"

"That I will. What show is yours?"

"The Sparling Combined Shows."

"That your car over there?"

"Yes--Car Three."

"You run it?"

"I do."

"Pretty young fellow to handle a car like that, aren't you?"

"I guess you are right. However, I am running it just the same."

"What is it you want me to do?"

"In the first place I want you to keep a close mouth. I do not want you to speak to a human being about my plans. There are some fellows that would like to know them. They must not."

The foreman grinned understandingly.

"I'm your man."

"I knew you were. You have a switch key of course?"

"Sure."

"Then I want you to bring your switch key here at half-past two o'clock tomorrow morning. You have crowbars in the tool house, have you not?"

"Yes."

"Bring two of them with you."

"What are you going to do?"

"Never mind now. I'll tell you when you come around in the morning. Do you think you can wake up in time?"

"Sure, I can."

"You may sleep on my car if you wish."

"No; I have a bunk in the tool house. I will come back and sleep there after supper."

"Excellent. Do you want an alarm clock?"

"No; I have one in the shanty. I often sleep there when I expect a call to go out on the road during the night."

"I am right, am I not, in my understanding that unless I get away on forty-two I shall not be able to leave here before noon tomorrow?"

"That's right. You are not going on forty-two, then?"

"I think not."

"The other fellows going on forty-two?"

"No; they will not be through billing here before sometime tomorrow."

The foreman grinned.

"I smell a rat," he said.

"Don't. It might not be healthful for you if you were to be too wise. Be on time and say nothing. How far is it to the next town?"

"Nigh onto twenty-five miles."

"All right. That's all. I will have your tickets ready for you when you come on in the morning. Good night, if I don't see you again until then."

All hands save Phil and Teddy went to bed early that night and the car was soon dark and silent. The late man from the country route did not get in until half-past one o'clock in the morning. He unloaded as quietly as possible, not knowing what plans of the manager he might disturb were he to make his presence known.

By this time every man of the crew was well aware that their young manager seldom was without some shrewd plan for outwitting his competitors, but these plans he ordinarily kept well to himself until he was ready to carry them out.

Phil busied himself during the night in posting his books, making out the pay-roll for the car, and writing the report sheet for the owner of the show.

Right on the minute at the appointed hour there came a light tap on the car window. Phil stepped out to the platform.

"I am ready, sir." It was the section foreman.

"Come inside," said Phil. "Do not make any noise, for the men are all asleep. I will awaken two of them soon, but I do not want those other car men to get awake, not for any price."

"Now, what is it you want to do?"

"You are sure there will be no more trains over this road in either direction tonight?" asked Phil.

"Not a train."

"That's good. Now I will tell you what I want you to do. I want you to open that switch to let us out on the main track."

The foreman opened his eyes.

"But how are you going to get out there?"

"I'll show you after you get the switch open. There is no grade up or down between here and the other side of the station, is there?"

"No; dead flat till you get ten rods beyond the station, then she drops."

Phil nodded thoughtfully.

"Get the crowbars while I call a couple of the men."

The Circus Boy went inside and gently awakened Billy Conley and Rosie, telling them to dress and report to the office at once.

The men made no protest. They knew their young manager was planning some new ruse by which to outwit his rivals. When they heard his plan they opened their eyes in wonder.

"Come on, now, and not a word nor a sound out of you, fellows!" commanded Phil.

Once outside, Phil threw off the brakes and then the foreman of the section gang brought his knowledge to bear on the situation. He directed the men to get their crowbars under the rear wheels of the coach. After several attempts they succeeded in prying the car ahead a few inches. After repeated efforts they got the car moving slowly.

Now the foreman took a third crowbar; jumping from one side to the other he relieved the men until the car was making very fair progress under its human power.

Teddy had been standing on the platform, rubbing his palms in high glee.

"Going to push her all the way to Marion like this?" he demanded.

"You keep still up there unless you are looking for trouble," warned Phil. "Get off the platform. Think we want to drag you along, too?"

Teddy hopped down, thrust his hands in his trousers pockets, and watched the operation of moving the heavy car.

It was slow work, but inch by inch Number Three crept nearer to the station.

"Let me know when we get right on the grade, so I can slap on the brakes," ordered Phil.

"I'll let you know. You'll know without my telling you, I reckon."

At last the car was at the desired point. Phil sprang to the platform and set the brakes, while the section man ran back and closed the switch.

"Here are your tickets," said Phil when the man returned. "And thank you very much."

"You're welcome, but don't you let on that I have helped you out. I will sure lose my job if you do."

"You need not worry. I do not forget a favor so easily as that."

"You better wait till daylight before you start," advised the foreman.

"Yes, I am going to. I do not want to take any more chances than I have to. There are enough as it is."

"Anything more I can do for you, sir?"

"No, thank you."

"Then, good night."

"Good night," answered Phil.

Teddy did not yet fully understand what his companion's plan might be. Billy, on the contrary, understood it fully.

"You beat anything I ever came across," Conley remarked in Phil's car as the two were standing at the side of the track in front of Number Three.

"Wait! Don't throw any flowers at me too soon. We have not done it yet. I understand there is a short up-grade about seven miles below here. If we get stalled on that we will be in a fine fix and likely to get smashed into ourselves. It looks to me like a storm. What do you think?"

"I think yes--thunderstorm. I saw the lightning a moment ago." "Good! I hope it storms. It will be a good cover to get away under."

"Slippery rails will be bad for our business, though," warned Billy.

"We shall have to take the chance."

They had not long to wait after that. Day soon dawned but the skies were dark and forbidding. As soon as it was light enough to see well, Phil began to make preparations for his unique trip.

"Now what are you going to do?" demanded Teddy.

"My dear boy, we are going to try to coast all the way to Marion. We may land in the ditch or we may get stalled, but I am not going to lie here and waste nearly a day. Let the other fellows spend the time here if they wish. I reckon they will be surprised in the morning, when they wake up and find Car Three has dropped off the map."

Teddy uttered a long whistle of surprise.

"Don't you ever find fault with me again for doing a trick like I played."

"What trick was that?" questioned Billy.

"Never mind. That's my secret. It isn't any of your affair," grumbled Teddy.

"Teddy, you get on the back platform. Keep your hand on the brake wheel every second of the time. Keep your ears open. When I jerk once sharply on the bell rope set the brakes tight. If I jerk it twice, just apply them a little to steady the car."

"Pull the bell rope? Huh! There isn't any bell."

"I know that, but you can hear the rope slap the top of the platform roof when I pull it. Now, get back there. Don't call out to me, but attend to your business.

I'll pull the cord when I am ready for you to release the brake. We must get away from here in a hurry."

Teddy hopped from the platform and ran to the rear, where he awaited the signal.

Phil's plan was a daring one. For twenty-five miles the road fell away at a sharp downgrade of sixty feet to the mile and in some places even greater. In one spot, as has already been stated, there was a sharp up-grade for a short distance.

It was Phil's purpose to coast the twenty-five miles in order to reach the next stand in time for the day's work. It was a risky undertaking. Besides the danger of a possible collision with an extra sent over the road, there was the added danger of the car getting beyond their control and toppling over into a ditch.

The Circus Boy had weighed all these chances well before starting on his undertaking.

"I guess we will be moving now," he said, giving the bell cord a pull, then throwing off the brake, Teddy performing the same service at the other end of the car.

Car Number Three did not start at once.

Phil and Billy jumped up and down on the platform in excitement.

"She's moving," exulted Phil. "We're off."

A faint "yee--ow!" from the rear platform was evidence that Teddy Tucker also had discovered this fact.

"That boy!" grumbled Phil.

At first the show car moved slowly; then little by little it began to gather headway. Rattling over switches, past lines of box cars, on past rows of houses that backed up against the railroad's right of way, they rumbled. A few moments later Car Three shot out into the open country at a lively rate of speed.

CHAPTER XX
ON A WILDCAT RUN

This is great!" cried Billy.

Phil Forrest, however, was keeping his eyes steadily on the shining rails ahead. All at once the storm broke. The lightning seemed to rend the heavens before them. Then the rain came down in a deluge.

So heavy was the rainfall that the young pilot could see only a few car lengths ahead of him. Instinctively he tightened the brakes slightly. The car was swaying giddily, not having a train with it to steady it.

"We ought to be near that grade the section man told us about," said Conley.

"Yes; I was just thinking of that. I guess I had better let her out, so we shall be sure to make it."

Phil threw off the brake wheel and Car Three shot ahead like a great projectile, rocking from side to side, moving at such high speed that the joints in the rails gave off a steady purring sound under the wheels.

The wildcat car struck the grade with a lurch and a bang, climbing it at a tremendous pace.

The two men on the front platform were compelled to hold on with their full strength, in order to keep from being hurled into the ditch beside the track.

"I hope Teddy is all right," shouted Phil.

Billy leaned out over the side looking back. Teddy, who was also leaning out, peering ahead regardless of the driving rain, waved a hand at him.

"Yes; you can't hurt *that* boy--"

Just then the car plunged over the crest of the hill and went thundering away down the steep grade.

By this time the men in the car had, one by one, been shaken awake by the car's terrific pace, and one by one they tumbled from their berths, quickly raising the curtains for a look outside.

What they saw was a driving storm and the landscape slipping past them at a higher speed than they ever had known before. Three of the men bolted to the front platform.

"What's the matter? Are we running away?" shouted a voice in Phil's car.

"Go back, fellows, and shut the door. Don't bother me. I'm making the next town."

The men retired to the car, sat down and looked at each other in blank amazement.

"Well, did you ever?" gasped Rosie.

"Never," answered the Missing Link, shaking his head helplessly. "He'll be the death of us yet."

"At least we'll be going some if we stay on this car."

"We *are* going some. We've been going some ever since the new Boss took hold of this car. I hope we don't hit anything. It'll be a year of Sundays for us, if we do."

"A good many years of 'em," muttered Rosie.

"I hear a train whistle!" shouted Billy, leaning toward Phil.

"I heard it," answered the boy calmly, beginning to tug at the brake wheel.

"Want any help?" asked Conley anxiously.

"No; you can't help me any." Phil had ceased twisting the wheel.

"What's the matter?"

"The wheels are slipping. The brakes will not hold them. If we are going to meet anything we might as well meet it properly," answered Phil calmly, whereupon he kicked the ratchet loose and spun the brake wheel about.

The car seemed to take a sudden leap forward.

Just then there came a rift in the clouds.

"Look!" cried Billy.

Phil leaned over the rail, peering into the mist.

The track, just a little way ahead of them, took a sudden bend around a high point of land. And on beyond the hill they saw the smoke of an engine belching up into the air like so many explosions.

"I guess that settles it," said the boy. His face was, perhaps, a little more pale than usual, but in no other way did he show any emotion.

"Shall we tell the men to jump, then go over ourselves?"

"No; we should all be killed. We will stay and see it through. The men are better off inside the car."

A yell from Teddy, sounding faint and far away, caused Billy to lean out and look back.

"Turn on your sand! Turn on your sand! She's slipping!" howled Teddy.

"We haven't any sand. D'you think this is a trolley car?"

Just then Teddy caught sight of the smoke ahead of them. He pointed. His voice seemed to fail him all at once.

"It looks as if we would get all the publicity we want in about a minute, Billy," said Phil, smiling easily. "We shall not be likely to know anything about it, though," he added.

Car Three swept around the bend.

"There they are!" cried Conley.

"Coming head on!" commented Phil. He seemed not in the least disturbed, despite the fact that he believed himself to be facing certain death.

Billy let out a yell of joy.

"They are on another track. They are not on these irons at all!" he shouted.

Phil had observed this at about the same instant. He saw something else, too. The road on which the train was approaching crossed his track at right angles. The other was a double track railroad, and the train was a fast express train, tearing along at high speed.

"We're safe!" breathed Billy, heaving a great sigh of relief.

"No, we are not. We are going to smash right into them, ***broadside,*** unless we can check our car enough to clear them."

"You think so?"

"I know so."

Billy groaned. His joy had been short-lived.

"Give Teddy the signal to put on the brakes. We will make another attempt to check her."

Phil threw himself into the task of turning the wheel, which he did in quick, short, spasmodic jerks, rather than by a steady application of the brakes.

The car slackened somewhat--hardly enough to be noticed.

"Tell Teddy to keep it up. You had better send one of the men back to help him."

Billy bellowed his command to the men inside.

"They see us. They are whistling to us."

"Yes."

Shriek after shriek rang out from the whistle of the approaching express train, the engineer of which jerked his throttle wide open in hopes of clearing the oncoming wildcat car.

Phil was still tugging desperately, but without any apparent nervousness, at the brake wheel. He finally ceased his efforts.

"I can't do any more," he said; then calmly leaned his arms on the wheel awaiting results.

Billy did not utter a word. He, too, possessed strong nerves.

The man and the boy stood there calmly watching the train ahead of them. Nearer and nearer to it did they draw. They could see the engineer and fireman leaning from their cab, looking back. Phil waved a hand to them, to which the engine crew responded in kind.

"Now for the smash, Billy, old boy!" muttered Phil with the smile that no peril seemed able to banish from his face.

"Yes; it's going to be a close shave."

The last car of the express train was now abreast of them. They seemed to be right upon it. So close were they that Phil thought he could stretch out a hand and touch it.

Suddenly it was whisked from before them as if by magic.

The engineer had given his engine its final burst of speed.

"Hang on tight!" shouted Phil. "We're going to sideswipe them now!"

"Off brakes!"

Billy gave the bell rope a tug.

Then came a crash, a grinding, jolting sound. It seemed as if the red car were being torn from end to end. Car Three careened, rocked and swayed, threatening every second to plunge from the rails over the embankment at that point.

As suddenly as it had come, the strain seemed to have been removed from it. Once more Number Three was thundering along over the rails.

"Yee--ow!" howled Teddy from the rear platform.

The men inside the car were not saying anything. They were slowly picking themselves up from the floor, where they had been hurled by the sudden shock. The interior of the car looked as if it had been struck by a tornado. The contents were piled in a confused heap at one end of the car, paste pots overturned, bedding stripped clean from the berths, lamps smashed, and great piles of paper scattered all over the place.

"Hooray!" yelled Billy in the excess of his joy. "We're saved."

"Yes," answered Phil with a grin. "It was a close call, though. I hope no one in the car is hurt. You had better go in and find out. I am afraid our car has been damaged."

Billy leaned over the side, looking back.

"Yes, we got a beauty of a sideswipe," he said.

The coupling and rear platform of the rear car on the express train had cut a deep gash in the side of Car Three, along half of its length.

"Any windows left?"

"I don't see anything that looks like glass left in them," laughed Conley.

"You watch the wheel a minute. I will go inside," said Phil.

He hurried into the car.

Phil could not repress a laugh at the scene that met his gaze.

"Hello, boys; what's going on in here?" called Phil.

"Say, Boss," spoke up Rosie the Pig. "If it's all the same to you, I think I'll get out and walk the rest of the way."

"Are we on time?" howled Teddy, poking his head in at the rear door.

"Better straighten the car out, for we should reach our town in a few minutes now--"

"I should say we would, at this gait," interrupted a voice.

"Then all hands will have to hustle out to work. I want to be out of the next stand sometime tonight. We go out on another road, so we shall not have to wait, unless something unforeseen occurs. Came pretty near having a smash-up, didn't we?" suggested Phil.

"Near?" The Missing Link's emotion was too great to permit him to finish the sentence.

The car bowled merrily along. In a short time the two men on the front platform were able to make out the outlines of the town ahead of them. The skies were clearing now, and shortly afterwards the sun burst through the clouds.

"All is sunshine," laughed Phil. "For a time it looked as if there would be a total eclipse," he added, grimly.

Billy gazed at him wonderingly.

"If I had your nerve I'd be a millionaire," said Billy in a low tone.

"You probably would break your neck the first thing you did," answered Phil with a short laugh.

They were now moving along on a level stretch of track. Phil set the brakes a little, and the car slowed down. In this way they glided easily into the station, where the Circus Boy brought the car to a stop directly in front of the telegraph office.

The station agent came out to see what it was that had come in so unexpectedly.

His amazement was great.

"Well, we are here," called Phil, stepping down from the platform. "I guess we are on time."

"Any orders?" shouted Teddy Tucker, dropping from the rear platform.

"Where--where did you fellows come from?"

"Salina."

"Where's your engine?"

"I'm the engine," spoke up Teddy. "Wasn't I behind, pushing Car Three all the way over?"

All hands set up a shout of laughter.

CHAPTER XXI
IN A PERILOUS POSITION

The story of Phil Forrest's brilliant and perilous dash quickly spread about the town. By six o'clock a great crowd had gathered about the station to get a look at the car and at the Circus Boy who had piloted her.

Phil was hustling about in search of an engine crew from the other road. He wanted his car moved from the main track, before some other train should come along and run into him, thus completing the wrecking that he already had so successfully begun.

In the meantime Teddy placed himself on view, parading up and down, looking wise and pompous. He always was willing to be admired. As soon as the newspaper offices were open he made haste to visit them, and the afternoon papers printed the story of Car Three's great wildcat dash, displaying the account under big, black headlines. The Sparling Shows got a full measure of publicity that day.

Teddy marked and wrapped copies of the papers containing the notice, mailing them back to the show for Mr. Sparling to read. On the margin of one of the papers so sent, Teddy wrote with a lead pencil, "no news today."

What the Circus Boy's idea of news really was it would be difficult to say.

Car Three had a fair field for most of the day. By the time the rivals got in there were few choice locations for billing left in the town.

The manager of the yellow car tried to induce the railroad authorities to proceed against Phil for the boy's action in taking his car over the division without authority. The road, however, refused to accede to the demand, and nothing ever was done about it. Perhaps Mr. Sparling had something to do with this, for telegrams were exchanged that day between the owner of the show and the division superintendent. In the meantime Phil did not trouble himself over the matter. He had too many other things to think of.

The next stand was to be in Oklahoma. Phil hoped that, by the time they reached there, they would be far enough ahead of the rival cars to shake them off entirely.

That afternoon he and Teddy went over town to look over the work. One of the first things to attract Phil's attention was a flag pole towering high above everything else in the city.

"Wouldn't I like to unfurl a Sparling banner from the top of that pole," exclaimed Phil, gazing up at the top. "How high is that pole?" he asked of a man standing near him.

"One hundred feet."

Teddy whistled softly.

"I wonder if I could get the consent of the town authorities to run some advertising matter up there?"

"Couldn't do it, even if you got the permission," answered the man.

"Why not?"

"There is no rope on the pole. It rotted off a year ago."

"That is too bad. I had already set my heart on billing the pole. It can be seen from all parts of the city, can it not?"

"Yes, and a long way out of the city at that."

"Come on, Teddy; let's not look at it. It makes me feel sad to think I cannot possess that pole."

"I wonder if you will ever be satisfied?" grumbled Teddy.

"Not as long as there is a spot on earth large enough for a Sparling one-sheet left uncovered."

"What will you give--what would you give, I mean, to have some banners put on top of the flag pole?"

"I would give fifty dollars and think I had got off very cheaply."

Teddy waxed thoughtful. Several times, that afternoon, he wandered over to the vicinity of the tall flag pole, and, leaning against a building, surveyed it critically.

After the fifth trip of this sort, the Circus Boy hurried back to the car. No one was on board save the porter. Teddy began rummaging about among the cloth banners, littering the floor with all sorts of rubbish in his feverish efforts to get what he wanted.

After considerable trouble he succeeded in laying out a gaudy assortment of banners. These he carefully stitched together until he had a completed flag or banner about fifty feet long.

"See here, Henry, don't you tell anybody what I have been doing, for you don't know."

"No, sir," agreed the porter.

Next Teddy provided himself with a light, strong rope. All his preparations completed, he once more strolled over town, where he joined Phil in watching the work. But he confided to his companion nothing of what he had been doing. Teddy Tucker's face wore its usual innocent expression.

That night, after supper, he called Billy Conley aside and confided to the assistant car manager what he had in mind.

"*Forget* it!" advised Billy with emphasis.

"I can't. I want to earn that fifty dollars."

"But if you break your neck what good will the fifty do you?"

"If I don't it will do me fifty dollars' worth of good," was the quick reply.

"How do you expect to do it?"

"I'll show you tonight. But we shall have to wait till most of the people are off the streets. You get away about ten o'clock, and don't let either Phil or any of the crew know where you are going. I will meet you on the other side of the station at ten o'clock sharp, provided I can get away from Phil."

"I don't like it, but I guess I am just enough of a good fellow to be willing to help you break your neck. Have you any family that you wish me to notify?"

"No one, unless it is January."

"Who's he?"

"My educated donkey."

"Oh, pshaw!" grumbled Billy.

At the appointed time Teddy made his exit from the car without attracting the attention of any of the crew. Phil was busy over his books, while the men were sitting on piles of paper, relating their experiences on the road.

Earlier in the evening Teddy had secreted his banners in what is known as the cellar, the large boxlike compartment under the car He now hastily gathered up his equipment and hurried to the station platform. Billy was already awaiting him there.

"You better give up this fool idea," warned Billy. "I don't want anything to do with it. You can go alone if you want to, but none of it for mine."

"Billy!"

"Well?"

"If you back down now, do you know what I'll do?"

"What will you do?"

"I'll give you the worst walloping you ever had in your life."

"You can't do it."

Teddy whipped off his coat.

"Come on; I'll show you."

Conley burst out laughing.

"The Boss says you are a hopeless case. I agree with him. Come on. I'll help you to break your neck."

They started off together. When they reached the pole, the pair dodged into a convenient doorway where they waited to make sure that they were not observed.

"I guess it is all right," said Teddy.

"How you going to get up there?"

"I brought a pair of climbers that I found in the car yesterday-- the kind those telephone linemen use to climb telephone poles with. Won't I go up, I guess *yes!*"

Teddy first strapped the banners over his shoulders, in such a way that they would not impede his progress; then he put on the climbers, Billy watching disapprovingly.

All was ready. With a final glance up and down the street Teddy strode from his hiding place.

He walked up the pole as if he were used to it. In a few minutes the watcher below could barely make him out in the faint moonlight.

"Look out, when you get up higher. The pole may be rotten," called Billy softly.

"All right. I'm up to the splice."

Here Teddy paused to rest, being now about halfway up the pole. Before going higher the Circus Boy prudently wrapped the small rope that he carried twice around the pole, forming a slip-noose. He made the free end fast around his body in case he should lose his footing.

This done, Teddy felt secure from a fall.

He worked his way slowly upward, creeping higher and higher, inch by inch, cautious but not in the least afraid, for Teddy was used to being high in the air.

Now and then he would pause to call down to the anxious Billy.

"Stand under to be ready to catch me if I fall," directed Tucker.

"Not much. You hit ground if you fall," jeered Conley.

Teddy's laugh floated down to him, carefree and happy. The Circus Boy was in his element.

Finally he managed to reach the top, or nearly to the top of the pole without mishap. The slender top of the flag pole swayed back and forth, like the mast of a ship in a rolling sea. It seemed to Teddy as if each roll would be his last.

He felt a slight dizziness, but it passed off quickly. In fact, he was too busy to give much heed to it. With nimble fingers he unpacked his roll of banners; and, in a few minutes, he was securing the long streamer to the pole, which he did by lacing it to the pole with leather thongs, through eyelets that he had sewed in the cloth.

In a few minutes the great banner fluttered to the breeze.

"Hurrah!" cried Teddy exultingly. "We're off!"

As he called out Teddy suddenly felt his footing give way beneath him. He had thrown too much weight on the climbers, and they had lost their grip.

CHAPTER XXII
A DASH FOR LIBERTY

H elp!"

"What is it?" cried Billy in alarm. "I'm hung up--hung down, I mean!"

"What--what's the matter, are you in trouble?"

"Yes, I'm hanging head down. I'm fast by the feet. Help me down!"

"Help you down? I can't help you. You will have to get out the best way you can. Can't you crawl up and free your feet?"

"No; go get Phil."

"Can you hold on?"

"I--I'll try. Go get Phil."

Conley dashed away as fast as he could run.

"I knew it, I knew it," he repeated at almost every bound.

Teddy's climbers had lost their grip in the rotting wood. Before he could recover himself he had tumbled backward. Fortunately the rope had clung to the pole; he was held fast but Teddy was hanging with his back against the pole, being powerless to help himself in the slightest degree. Again, he was afraid that, were he to stir about, the rope, which had slipped down and drawn tight about his ankles, might suddenly slide down the pole and dash him to his death.

Not many minutes had elapsed before Phil and Conley came running back. Phil, at the suggestion of the assistant manager, had brought a pair of climbers with him, Billy explaining, as they ran, the fix that the Circus Boy was in.

For a wonder, all the disturbance had attracted no attention on the street.

"Are you all right?" called Phil as he ran to the spot.

"N--no; I'm all wrong," came the answer from above. "All the blood in my body is in my head. I'm going to burst in a minute."

Phil wasted no words. Quickly strapping on his climbers, he began shinning up the pole, which he took much faster than Teddy had done, for the situation was critical.

"Hurry up! Think I want to stay here all night?"

"I'm coming. Hang on a few moments longer," panted Phil, for the exertion was starting the perspiration all over his body.

At last he reached the spot where Teddy was hanging head down.

"Well, you have got yourself into a nice fix!" growled Phil.

"I got the banners up," retorted Teddy.

Phil cast his eyes aloft, and there, above his head, floated the gaudy banners of the Sparling Show.

"Great!" he muttered. "But you are lucky if it doesn't cost you your life and perhaps mine, too. Now, when I place this rope in your hands, you hang on to it for all you are worth. I will make it fast above, and I think I shall have to cut the rope that holds your feet. I see no other way to get you down."

"What, and let me drop? No, you don't."

"I shall not let you drop if I can help it. Can't you manage to get a grip on the pole with your arms?"

"If I were facing the other way, I might."

"Twist yourself. Aren't you enough of a circus man to do a contortion act as simple as that?"

Teddy thought he was. At least, he was willing to try, and he succeeded very well, throwing a firm grip about the pole.

Phil cautiously climbed above his companion. None save a trained aerial worker could have accomplished such a feat, but the Circus Boy managed it without mishap. He then made fast a rope about the pole above the place where Teddy's rope was secured, drawing it tight above a slight projection on the pole itself, where part of a knot had been left.

Phil had not secured himself as Teddy had done, but he felt no fear of falling as long as he had one arm about the pole. He might slip, but even then the principal danger to be apprehended was that he might carry Teddy down with him.

"Pass the rope about your body," directed Phil.

"Which rope?"

"My rope--*this* rope," answered Phil, raising and lowering the rope that Teddy might make no mistake. "If you get the wrong one you will take a fine tumble. Got it?"

"Yes."

"All right. When you have secured it about your body let me know."

"I've got it."

"Have you also got a firm grip on the pole?"

"Yes."

"Then look out. I am going to cut your feet loose. Are you ready?"

"All ready!"

Phil severed the rope that held Teddy's feet, and the boy did a half turn in the air, his feet suddenly flopping over until he found himself in an upright position. But the twist of the body had given him a fearful wrench, drawing a loud "ouch!" from Teddy. To add to his troubles Tucker found himself unable to move.

"I'm tied up in a hard knot," he wailed.

"What's the trouble?"

"I'm all twisted. I can't wiggle a toe."

"Well, you don't have to wiggle your toes, do you?"

Phil found the work of extricating his companion a more difficult matter than he had expected, and to set Teddy free it was necessary to cut the rope again.

This time the cutting was followed instantly by a wild yell.

Teddy shot down to the splice in the pole, where he struck the crosspiece with a jolt that shook the pole from top to bottom; but, fortunately, his arms were about the pole and the crosspiece had kept him from plunging to the ground many feet below.

"Are you all right?" called Phil.

"No; I'm killed."

"Lucky you didn't break the pole, at any rate."

"Break the pole? Break the pole?" yelled Teddy, half in anger, half in pain. "What do I care about the pole? I've broken myself. I won't be able to sit down again this season. Oh, why did I ever come with this outfit?"

"Hurry and get down. We shall have the whole town awake if you keep up that racket."

Phil let himself down to where Teddy sat rubbing himself and growling.

"Go on down. You are not hurt," commanded Phil.

"I am, I tell you."

"Well, are you going to stay up here all night?"

Teddy pulled himself together, preparing for the descent.

"Can you get down alone? If not I will tie a rope to you to protect you."

"No; you keep away from me. I'll get down if you let me alone."

"Teddy Tucker, you are an ungrateful boy."

"I'm a sore boy; that's what I am. Don't speak to me till I get down again. Then I'll talk with you and I'll have something to say, too. I want that fifty dollars for putting the banner up, too."

"Well, wait till you get down, anyhow," retorted Phil impatiently.

Teddy made his way down, muttering and growling every foot of the way, followed by Phil at a safe distance, the latter chuckling and laughing at Teddy's rage.

Young Tucker had nearly reached the base of the pole, when once more he missed his footing.

Billy Conley was just below him, ready to assist, when Teddy landed on him, both going down together.

Teddy uttered a yell that could have been heard more than a block away.

As the two struggled to get up, both Teddy and Billy threatening each other, rapid footsteps were heard approaching them down the street. In a moment they saw the flash of a policeman's shield.

"We're caught!" cried Conley. "Run for it!"

"Halt!" commanded the officer. He was almost upon them now. Phil was still up the pole, where he clung, awaiting the result of the surprise below.

"What does this mean?" demanded the bluecoat.

"It means you are it!" howled Teddy, bolting between the officer's legs, causing the bluecoat to fall flat upon the ground.

"Run! Run!" howled Teddy.

Phil sprang from the pole and all hands made a lively sprint for the car.

CHAPTER XXIII
THE DESERTED VILLAGE

But Teddy had distinguished himself. When the town awakened next morning there were loud clamorings for the arrest of the showman who had dared to unfurl a circus advertisement from the top of the city's flag pole. The showmen guilty of the deed were many, many miles away by that time, engaged in other similar occupations.

At McAlister, a booming western town, the opposition were still hard on the heels of Car Three. Try as he would Phil Forrest was able to shake them off no longer than a few hours at a time.

A new plan occurred to him, and immediately upon his arrival at McAlister he wired Mr. Sparling to send a brigade into the next town ahead, to bill the place, in order that Car Three might make a jump and get away from its rivals.

A brigade, it should be known, is a crew of men that does not travel on a special car. They go by regular train, traveling as other passengers do, dropping off and billing a town here and there, as directed by wire.

The answer came back that the brigade would relieve him at the next stand.

While this had been going on young Tucker had been listening to a most interesting tale of a deserted town some twenty miles beyond where they were then working. The deserted town was known as Owls' Valley. It had been a prosperous little city up to within two months previous, when, for reasons that Teddy did not learn, the inhabitants had taken a sudden leave.

This information set Teddy Tucker to thinking. A deserted village? He wished that he might see it. He had heard of deserted villages, and this one was of more than ordinary interest, because, the moment he heard of it, a plan presented itself to his fertile mind.

"I'll bet they will not only nibble at the bait, but will swallow it whole," he decided exultingly after he had thoroughly gone over the plan, sitting off by himself on a pile of railroad iron. "I'll take Billy into my confidence. Billy will spread the word, and then we shall see what will happen."

When Billy came in Teddy called him aside and outlined his plan.

Billy returned from the conference grinning broadly, but Teddy was serious and thoughtful.

However, he decided not to tell Phil what he had done. Perhaps Phil might not approve of it. Phil was so peculiar that he might visit the rival cars and tell them that certain information they had obtained was not correct.

Be that as it may, a few hours later three car managers visited the station, leaving orders that their cars were to be switched off at Owls' Valley.

"That fellow, Forrest, thought he would play a smart trick on us and slip into a town not down on his route, where he was going to have all the billing to himself," said the manager of the yellow car, late that evening.

"Where is Owls' Valley?" asked one of his men.

"About twenty miles west of here. It will be a short run. He will be a very much surprised young man when he wakes up in the morning and finds us lying on the siding with him."

The train to which the cars were to be attached was not to leave until sometime after midnight. When it finally came in all the advertising car crews were in bed and asleep. Teddy Tucker, however, was not only wide awake, but outside at that.

"Couple us up next to your rear car, and put the other fellows on the rear if you will," he said to the conductor. "They are going to Owls' Valley, but we are going through. Please say nothing to them about what I have told you. Here's a pass for the circus."

The rest was easy. Soon the train was rumbling away, with Teddy the happiest mortal on it. But he did not go to bed. Not Teddy! He sat up to make sure that his plans did not miscarry. Owls' Valley was reached in due time, and the Circus Boy was outside to make sure that no mistake was made. He did not propose that Car Three should, by any slip, be sidetracked at the deserted village.

Very shortly afterwards they were again on their way, and Teddy went to bed well satisfied with his night's work. When the men woke up early next morning a new train crew was in charge, for the advertising car was making a long run.

Phil was the first to awaken. As was customary with him he stepped to the window and peered out.

"Why, we seem to be the last car on the train. There were three opposition cars behind us when we started out last night. I wonder what that means?"

Quickly dressing, he went out on the platform. Leaning over he looked ahead. Car Three was the only show car on the train.

"That is queer. I do not understand it at all."

Hurrying in to the main part of the car Phil called to the men.

"Do any of you know what has become of the opposition?" he asked.

"Why, aren't they on behind?"

"No one is on behind. We are the last car. Those fellows have stolen a march on us somewhere. I can't imagine where they dropped off, though; can you?"

"Maybe they have switched off on another road," suggested a voice.

"No other road they could switch off on. There is something more to this than appears on the surface. I'll go forward and ask the conductor."

Phil did so, but the conductor could give him no information. Car Three was the only show car on the train when the present conductor had taken charge.

Phil was more puzzled than ever. He consulted his route list, to make sure that he himself had not made a mistake and skipped a town that he should have billed. No; there was only one town he had missed, and that was the one the brigade was to work.

About this time Teddy sat up, rubbing his eyes sleepily.

"What's up?" he inquired, noting that his companion was troubled.

"That is what I should like to know," answered Phil absently.

"Tell me about it. Anything gone wrong?"

"I don't know. The opposition has disappeared."

"Disappeared?"

"Yes; they disappeared during the night, and I cannot imagine where they have gone. They must have dropped in on some town that we should have made, and I am worried."

Teddy pulled up a window shade and studied the landscape for several minutes.

"Curious, isn't it?" he mumbled.

"Yes."

"I might make a guess where they went, Phil."

"You might guess?"

"That's what I said."

"Where do you think they have gone?"

"If I were to make a long-range guess, I should say that perhaps the cars of the opposition were sidetracked at Owls' Valley."

"Where is that? I never heard of the place."

"That, my dear sir, is the deserted village. Lonesome Town, they ought to call it."

"Where is it?"

"About twenty miles from the last stand; and, if they are there, they will be likely to stay there for sometime to come."

Phil had wheeled about, studying his companion keenly.

"You seem to know a great deal about the movements of the enemy. How does it happen that you are so well posted, Teddy Tucker?"

"I was hanging around the station when they gave the order to have their cars dropped off there," answered Teddy, avoiding the keen gaze of his companion and superior.

"Did you know the place was deserted?"

Teddy nodded.

"Did *they?*"

Teddy shook his head.

"How did they happen to order their cars dropped off there?"

"I--I guess somebody must have told them that--I guess maybe they thought we were going there."

"Thought we were going there?"

"Yes."

"Why?"

"Oh, because."

A light was beginning to dawn upon the young car manager. He surveyed Teddy from beneath half closed eyelids. Tucker grew restless under the critical examination.

"Say, stop your looking at me that way."

"Why?"

"You make me nervous. Stop it, I say!"

"Tell me all about it, Teddy," urged Phil, trying hard to make his tone stern.

"Tell you about what?"

"Why the opposition happened to think we were going to Owls' Valley."

"Maybe they just imagined it."

"And maybe they did not. You are mixed up in this, in some way, and I want to know all about it, Teddy Tucker. I hope you have done nothing dishonorable. Of course I am glad the other fellows are out of our way, but I want to know how. Come, be frank with me. You are avoiding the question. Remember I am the manager of this car; I am responsible for all that is done on it. Out with it!"

Teddy fidgeted.

"Well, it was this way. Somebody told them--"

"Well, told them what?" urged Phil.

"Told them they heard we were going to bill Owls' Valley."

"So, that's it, eh?"

Teddy nodded again.

"Did you give out any such information as that?"

Teddy shook his head.

"Who did?"

"I won't tell. You can't make me tell," retorted the Circus Boy belligerently.

"But you were responsible for the rumor getting out?"

Teddy did not answer.

"And those poor fellows are lying there on the siding, twenty miles from the nearest telegraph office?"

"I guess so." Tucker grinned broadly.

"And how are they going to get out?"

"Walk!"

Phil broke out into a roar of laughter.

"Oh, Teddy, what am I going to do with you? Do you know you have done very wrong?"

"No, I don't. The trouble with you is that you don't appreciate a good thing when you get it. You were wishing you could get rid of the opposition cars, weren't you?"

"Yes, but--"

"Well, you're rid of them, aren't you?"

"Yes, but--"

"And I got rid of them for you."

"Yes, but as I was saying--"

"Then what have you got to raise such a row about? You got your wish."

Teddy curled up and began studying the landscape again.

"I admire your zeal young man, but your methods are open to severe criticism. First you imperil the lives of three carloads of men by cutting them loose from the train; then you climb a flag pole, nearly losing your own life in the attempt, and now you have lured three carloads of men to a deserted village, where you have lost them. Oh, I've got to laugh--I can't help it!" And Phil did laugh, disturbed as he was over Teddy Tucker's repeated violation of what Phil believed to be the right and honorable way of doing business.

"Billy!" called Phil.

Mr. Conley responded promptly.

"I am not asking any questions. I do not want to know any more than I do about this business. I already know more than I wish I knew. I want to say, however, that when any more plans are made, any schemes hatched for outwitting our rivals, I shall appreciate being made acquainted with such plans before they are put into practice."

Teddy looked up in amazement. He had not the remotest idea that Phil even suspected who had been his accomplice. But the car manager had no need to be told. He was too shrewd not to suspect at once who it was that had carried out Teddy's suggestions and sidetracked the opposition where they would not get out for at least a whole day.

"Yes, sir," answered Billy meekly.

"I understand that the opposition are where they are likely to stay for sometime to come?"

"Yes, sir; so I understand."

"Oh, you do, eh?"

"Yes, sir."

"You know all about it? Well, I thought as much. But I am sorry you have admitted it. That necessitates my reading you a severe lecture."

This Phil did, laying down the law as Conley never had supposed the Circus Boy could do. Billy repeated the lecture to the rest of the crew, later on, and all agreed that Phil Forrest, the young advance agent, had left nothing unsaid. Phil's stock rose correspondingly. A man who could "call down" his crew properly was a real car manager.

While the Sparling Show profited by Teddy's ruse, Phil felt unhappy that his advantage had come by reason of the falsehood that Teddy had told; and that night Phil read his young friend a severe lecture.

"If I find you doing a trick like that again," concluded Phil, "you close there and then."

CHAPTER XXIV
CONCLUSION

Who is the man in charge of Sparling Advance Car Number Three?" demanded Mr. Starr, manager of "The Greatest Show on Earth."

"A young fellow named Forrest. That is all I know about him," answered the treasurer of the show.

"He used to be a performer and a good one, too," spoke up the assistant manager.

This conversation took place in the office tent of the show that Phil Forrest had been fighting almost ever since he took charge of Car Three.

"He is one of the best bareback riders who ever entered the forty-two foot ring," continued the assistant manager.

"What has he ever done before? I never heard of him."

"He has been with Sparling, I think, about five years. I understand he never did any circus work before that."

"I want that young man," announced the general manager decisively.

"Probably money will get him," smiled the treasurer.

"I do not wish to do anything to offend Sparling, for he is an old friend, and one of the best showmen in the country. I'll write him today, and see what he has to say. That young man, Forrest, or whatever his name may be, is giving us more trouble than we ever had before. He is practically putting our men all out of business. We shall have to change our route, or close, if he keeps on heading off our advance cars."

"It has come to a pretty pass, if a green boy with no previous experience is to defeat us. What is the matter with our advance men?" demanded the assistant manager.

"That is what I should like to know," answered Mr. Starr. "I will write Sparling today about this matter."

Weeks had passed and Car Three had worked its way across the plains, on into the mountainous country. Car managers had again been changed on the yellow car; another car had been sent in ahead of Phil, but to no better purpose than before.

Car Three moved on, making one brilliant dash after another, sometimes winning out by the narrowest margin and apparently by pure luck. Still, Phil Forrest and his loyal crew were never caught napping and were never headed off for more than a day at a time.

The season was drawing to a close. One day Phil received a wire from Mr. Sparling reading:

"Close at Deming, New Mexico, September fifteen."

"Boys, the end is in sight; and I, for one, shall be glad when we are through," announced Phil, appearing in the men's part of the car, where he read the telegram from the owner of the show.

The men set up a cheer.

"Now let's drive the other fellows off the map during these remaining two weeks."

How those men did work! No man on that car overslept during the rest of the trip. Phil seemed not to know the meaning of the word "tired." All hours of the night found him on duty, either watching the movements of his car or laying out work ahead, planning and scheming to outwit his rivals.

At last Car Three rolled into the station at Deming. It was a warm, balmy Fall day.

"Now burn the town up with your paper, boys," commanded Phil, after they had finished their breakfast. "Come in early tonight. I want all hands to drop paste pots and brushes tonight, and take dinner with me. It will not be at a contract hotel, either. Dinner at eight o'clock."

"Hooray!" exclaimed Teddy. "A real feed for once, fellows! No more meals at The Sign of the Tin Spoon this season!"

The crew of Car Three were not slow about getting in that night. Every man was on time. They dodged out of the car with bundles under their arms, got a refreshing bath, and spick and span in tailor-made clothes and clean linen, they presented themselves at the car just before eight o'clock.

"Hello! You boys do not look natural," hailed Phil, with a laugh. "But come along; I know you are hungry, and so am I."

The Circus Boy had arranged for a fine dinner at the leading hotel of the city, where he had engaged a private dining room for the evening.

It was a jolly meal. Everyone was happy in the consciousness of work well done, in the knowledge that they had outrivaled every opposition car that had been sent into their field.

The dinner was nearing its close when Phil rose and rapped for order.

"Boys," he said, "you have done great work. You have been loyal, and without your help I should have made a miserable failure of this work. You know how green I was, how little I really know about the advance work yet--"

Someone laughed.

"You need not laugh. I know it, whether you boys do or not. I asked you to dine with Teddy and myself here tonight, that I might tell you these things and thank you. If ever I am sent in advance again I hope you boys will be with me, every one of you."

"You bet we will!" shouted the men in chorus.

"And let me add that Mr. Sparling is not ungrateful for the work you have done this season. He has asked me to present you with a small expression of his appreciation. Teddy, will you please pass these envelopes to the boys? You will find their names written on the envelopes."

Tucker quickly distributed the little brown envelopes.

The men shouted. Each envelope held a crisp, new fifty-dollar bill.

"Three cheers for Boss Sparling!" cried Rosie the Pig, springing to his feet, waving the bill above his head.

The cheers were given with a will.

"I will bid you good-bye tonight," continued Phil. "Teddy and myself will take a late train for the East, after we get through. We are going back to join the show until it closes--"

"Wait a minute, Boss," interrupted Billy Conley, rising. "This show isn't over yet."

"The Band Concert in the main tent is about to begin."

Phil glanced at him inquiringly.

"All the natural curiosities, including the Missing Link and the Human Pig, will be on view. Take your seats in the center ring, immediately after the performance closes!"

Billy drew a package from his pocket and placed it on the table before him.

"Boss, the fellows have asked me to present to you a little expression of their good will--to the greatest advance agent that ever hit the iron trail. You've made us work like all possessed, but we love you almost to death, just the same. I present this gift to you with our compliments, Boss, and here also is a little remembrance for our friend, Spotted Horse, otherwise known as Teddy Tucker."

Billy sat down, and Phil, rising, accepted the gift. Opening the package he found a handsome gold watch and chain, his initials set in the back of the watch case in diamonds.

"Oh, boys, why did you do it?" gasped Phil, in an unsteady voice.

"I've got a diamond stick pin!" shouted Teddy triumphantly.

Phil's eyes were moist.

"Why--why did you--"

" 'Cause--'cause you're the best fellow that ever lived! Say, quit lookin' at me like that, or I'll blubber right out," stammered Billy, hastily pushing back his chair and walking over to the window.

"For he's a jolly good fellow!" struck up Rosie the Pig. All joined in the chorus, while Phil sat down helplessly, unable to say a word.

On the second morning thereafter the Circus Boys rejoined the Great Sparling Shows, where they were welcomed right royally. Teddy insisted in going on with his mule act that same day.

Even the donkey was glad to see Teddy. January evinced his pleasure at having his young master with him again by promptly kicking young Tucker through the side wall of the pad room, nearly breaking the Circus Boy's neck.

That day a letter came to Phil from The Greatest Show on Earth. After reading it, Phil hastened to his employer.

"I have a letter offering us both a contract with The Greatest for next season. What do you think of that, Mr. Sparling?" asked Phil with sparkling eyes.

Mr. Sparling did not appear to be surprised.

"Well, what are you going to do about it?"

"Refuse it, of course. I prefer to stay with you."

"And I prefer to have you."

"I thought you would."

"But I shall ask you to accept; in fact, I wish you to do so. You will find the experience valuable. When you finish your season with the big show I shall have something of great importance to communicate to you, if you wish to return to us."

"Wish to?"

"Yes; so wire on your acceptance right away, my boy, then you and I will have a long talk."

So it was left. Phil went on with the show during the remaining four weeks, then the boys turned their faces homeward, where they planned to put in a busy winter practicing and studying.

Despite their reluctance to leave Mr. Sparling for a season, they were looking forward to the coming Spring when they were to join the other show. Their experiences there will be related in a following volume, entitled, "THE CIRCUS BOYS AT THE TOP; Or, Bossing the Greatest Show of All."

The Codes Of Hammurabi And Moses
W. W. Davies

The discovery of the Hammurabi Code is one of the greatest achievements of archaeology, and is of paramount interest, not only to the student of the Bible, but also to all those interested in ancient history...

Religion   **ISBN: *1-59462-338-4***

QTY

Pages:132
MSRP $12.95

The Theory of Moral Sentiments
Adam Smith

This work from 1749. contains original theories of conscience amd moral judgment and it is the foundation for systemof morals.

Philosophy **ISBN: *1-59462-777-0***

QTY

Pages:536
MSRP $19.95

Jessica's First Prayer
Hesba Stretton

In a screened and secluded corner of one of the many railway-bridges which span the streets of London there could be seen a few years ago, from five o'clock every morning until half past eight, a tidily set-out coffee-stall, consisting of a trestle and board, upon which stood two large tin cans, with a small fire of charcoal burning under each so as to keep the coffee boiling during the early hours of the morning when the work-people were thronging into the city on their way to their daily toil...

Childrens   **ISBN: *1-59462-373-2***

QTY

Pages:84
MSRP $9.95

My Life and Work
Henry Ford

Henry Ford revolutionized the world with his implementation of mass production for the Model T automobile. Gain valuable business insight into his life and work with his own auto-biography... "We have only started on our development of our country we have not as yet, with all our talk of wonderful progress, done more than scratch the surface. The progress has been wonderful enough but..."

Biographies/   **ISBN: *1-59462-198-5***

QTY

Pages:300
MSRP $21.95

The Art of Cross-Examination
Francis Wellman

QTY

I presume it is the experience of every author, after his first book is published upon an important subject, to be almost overwhelmed with a wealth of ideas and illustrations which could readily have been included in his book, and which to his own mind, at least, seem to make a second edition inevitable. Such certainly was the case with me; and when the first edition had reached its sixth impression in five months, I rejoiced to learn that it seemed to my publishers that the book had met with a sufficiently favorable reception to justify a second and considerably enlarged edition. ...

Pages:412

Reference　　ISBN: *1-59462-647-2*　　*MSRP $19.95*

On the Duty of Civil Disobedience
Henry David Thoreau

QTY

Thoreau wrote his famous essay, On the Duty of Civil Disobedience, as a protest against an unjust but popular war and the immoral but popular institution of slave-owning. He did more than write—he declined to pay his taxes, and was hauled off to gaol in consequence. Who can say how much this refusal of his hastened the end of the war and of slavery ?

Law　　　ISBN: *1-59462-747-9*　　**Pages:48**

MSRP $7.45

Dream Psychology Psychoanalysis for Beginners
Sigmund Freud

QTY

Sigmund Freud, born Sigismund Schlomo Freud (May 6, 1856 - September 23, 1939), was a Jewish-Austrian neurologist and psychiatrist who co-founded the psychoanalytic school of psychology. Freud is best known for his theories of the unconscious mind, especially involving the mechanism of repression; his redefinition of sexual desire as mobile and directed towards a wide variety of objects; and his therapeutic techniques, especially his understanding of transference in the therapeutic relationship and the presumed value of dreams as sources of insight into unconscious desires.

Pages:196

Psychology　ISBN: *1-59462-905-6*　　*MSRP $15.45*

The Miracle of Right Thought
Orison Swett Marden

QTY

Believe with all of your heart that you will do what you were made to do. When the mind has once formed the habit of holding cheerful, happy, prosperous pictures, it will not be easy to form the opposite habit. It does not matter how improbable or how far away this realization may see, or how dark the prospects may be, if we visualize them as best we can, as vividly as possible, hold tenaciously to them and vigorously struggle to attain them, they will gradually become actualized, realized in the life. But a desire, a longing without endeavor, a yearning abandoned or held indifferently will vanish without realization.

Pages:360

Self Help　　　　ISBN: *1-59462-644-8*　　*MSRP $25.45*

QTY

The Rosicrucian Cosmo-Conception Mystic Christianity *by Max Heindel* ISBN: *1-59462-188-8* **$38.95**
The Rosicrucian Cosmo-conception is not dogmatic, neither does it appeal to any other authority than the reason of the student. It is: not controversial, but is: sent forth in the, hope that it may help to clear... New Age/Religion Pages 646

Abandonment To Divine Providence *by Jean-Pierre de Caussade* ISBN: *1-59462-228-0* **$25.95**
"The Rev. Jean Pierre de Caussade was one of the most remarkable spiritual writers of the Society of Jesus in France in the 18th Century. His death took place at Toulouse in 1751. His works have gone through many editions and have been republished... Inspirational/Religion Pages 400

Mental Chemistry *by Charles Haanel* ISBN: *1-59462-192-6* **$23.95**
Mental Chemistry allows the change of material conditions by combining and appropriately utilizing the power of the mind. Much like applied chemistry creates something new and unique out of careful combinations of chemicals the mastery of mental chemistry... New Age Pages 354

The Letters of Robert Browning and Elizabeth Barret Barrett 1845-1846 vol II ISBN: *1-59462-193-4* **$35.95**
by Robert Browning and Elizabeth Barrett Biographies Pages 596

Gleanings In Genesis (volume I) *by Arthur W. Pink* ISBN: *1-59462-130-6* **$27.45**
Appropriately has Genesis been termed "the seed plot of the Bible" for in it we have, in germ form, almost all of the great doctrines which are afterwards fully developed in the books of Scripture which follow... Religion/Inspirational Pages 420

The Master Key *by L. W. de Laurence* ISBN: *1-59462-001-6* **$30.95**
In no branch of human knowledge has there been a more lively increase of the spirit of research during the past few years than in the study of Psychology, Concentration and Mental Discipline. The requests for authentic lessons in Thought Control, Mental Discipline and... New Age/Business Pages 422

The Lesser Key Of Solomon Goetia *by L. W. de Laurence* ISBN: *1-59462-092-X* **$9.95**
This translation of the first book of the "Lemegton" which is now for the first time made accessible to students of Talismanic Magic was done, after careful collation and edition, from numerous Ancient Manuscripts in Hebrew, Latin, and French... New Age/Occult Pages 92

Rubaiyat Of Omar Khayyam *by Edward Fitzgerald* ISBN:*1-59462-332-5* **$13.95**
Edward Fitzgerald, whom the world has already learned, in spite of his own efforts to remain within the shadow of anonymity, to look upon as one of the rarest poets of the century, was born at Bredfield, in Suffolk, on the 31st of March, 1809. He was the third son of John Purcell... Music Pages 172

Ancient Law *by Henry Maine* ISBN: *1-59462-128-4* **$29.95**
The chief object of the following pages is to indicate some of the earliest ideas of mankind, as they are reflected in Ancient Law, and to point out the relation of those ideas to modern thought. Religion/History Pages 452

Far-Away Stories *by William J. Locke* ISBN: *1-59462-129-2* **$19.45**
"Good wine needs no bush, but a collection of mixed vintages does. And this book is just such a collection. Some of the stories I do not want to remain buried for ever in the museum files of dead magazine-numbers an author's not unpardonable vanity..." Fiction Pages 272

Life of David Crockett *by David Crockett* ISBN: *1-59462-250-7* **$27.45**
"Colonel David Crockett was one of the most remarkable men of the times in which he lived. Born in humble life, but gifted with a strong will, an indomitable courage, and unremitting perseverance... Biographies/New Age Pages 424

Lip-Reading *by Edward Nitchie* ISBN: *1-59462-206-X* **$25.95**
Edward B. Nitchie, founder of the New York School for the Hard of Hearing, now the Nitchie School of Lip-Reading, Inc, wrote "LIP-READING Principles and Practice". The development and perfecting of this meritorious work on lip-reading was an undertaking... How-to Pages 400

A Handbook of Suggestive Therapeutics, Applied Hypnotism, Psychic Science ISBN: *1-59462-214-0* **$24.95**
by Henry Munro Health/New Age/Health/Self-help Pages 376

A Doll's House: and Two Other Plays *by Henrik Ibsen* ISBN: *1-59462-112-8* **$19.95**
Henrik Ibsen created this classic when in revolutionary 1848 Rome. Introducing some striking concepts in playwriting for the realist genre, this play has been studied the world over. Fiction/Classics/Plays 308

The Light of Asia *by sir Edwin Arnold* ISBN: *1-59462-204-3* **$13.95**
In this poetic masterpiece, Edwin Arnold describes the life and teachings of Buddha. The man who was to become known as Buddha to the world was born as Prince Gautama of India but he rejected the worldly riches and abandoned the reigns of power when... Religion/History/Biographies Pages 170

The Complete Works of Guy de Maupassant *by Guy de Maupassant* ISBN: *1-59462-157-8* **$16.95**
"For days and days, nights and nights, I had dreamed of that first kiss which was to consecrate our engagement, and I knew not on what spot I should put my lips..." Fiction/Classics Pages 240

The Art of Cross-Examination *by Francis L. Wellman* ISBN: *1-59462-309-0* **$26.95**
Written by a renowned trial lawyer, Wellman imparts his experience and uses case studies to explain how to use psychology to extract desired information through questioning. How-to/Science/Reference Pages 408

Answered or Unanswered? *by Louisa Vaughan* ISBN: *1-59462-248-5* **$10.95**
Miracles of Faith in China Religion Pages 112

The Edinburgh Lectures on Mental Science (1909) *by Thomas* ISBN: *1-59462-008-3* **$11.95**
This book contains the substance of a course of lectures recently given by the writer in the Queen Street Hall, Edinburgh. Its purpose is to indicate the Natural Principles governing the relation between Mental Action and Material Conditions... New Age/Psychology Pages 148

Ayesha *by H. Rider Haggard* ISBN: *1-59462-301-5* **$24.95**
Verily and indeed it is the unexpected that happens! Probably if there was one person upon the earth from whom the Editor of this, and of a certain previous history, did not expect to hear again... Classics Pages 380

Ayala's Angel *by Anthony Trollope* ISBN: *1-59462-352-X* **$29.95**
The two girls were both pretty, but Lucy who was twenty-one who supposed to be simple and comparatively unattractive, whereas Ayala was credited, as her Bombwhat romantic name might show, with poetic charm and a taste for romance. Ayala when her father died was nineteen... Fiction Pages 484

The American Commonwealth *by James Bryce* ISBN: *1-59462-286-8* **$34.45**
An interpretation of American democratic political theory. It examines political mechanics and society from the perspective of Scotsman James Bryce Politics Pages 572

Stories of the Pilgrims *by Margaret P. Pumphrey* ISBN: *1-59462-116-0* **$17.95**
This book explores pilgrims religious oppression in England as well as their escape to Holland and eventual crossing to America on the Mayflower, and their early days in New England... History Pages 268

QTY

The Fasting Cure *by Sinclair Upton*   ISBN: *1-59462-222-1*   **$13.95**
In the Cosmopolitan Magazine for May, 1910, and in the Contemporary Review (London) for April, 1910, I published an article dealing with my experiences in fasting. I have written a great many magazine articles, but never one which attracted so much attention... New Age/Self Help/Health Pages 164

Hebrew Astrology *by Sepharial*   ISBN: *1-59462-308-2*   **$13.45**
In these days of advanced thinking it is a matter of common observation that we have left many of the old landmarks behind and that we are now pressing forward to greater heights and to a wider horizon than that which represented the mind-content of our progenitors... Astrology Pages 144

Thought Vibration or The Law of Attraction in the Thought World   ISBN: *1-59462-127-6*   **$12.95**
by William Walker Atkinson   Psychology/Religion Pages 144

Optimism *by Helen Keller*   ISBN: *1-59462-108-X*   **$15.95**
Helen Keller was blind, deaf, and mute since 19 months old, yet famously learned how to overcome these handicaps, communicate with the world, and spread her lectures promoting optimism. An inspiring read for everyone... Biographies/Inspirational Pages 84

Sara Crewe *by Frances Burnett*   ISBN: *1-59462-360-0*   **$9.45**
In the first place, Miss Minchin lived in London. Her home was a large, dull, tall one, in a large, dull square, where all the houses were alike, and all the sparrows were alike, and where all the door-knockers made the same heavy sound... Childrens/Classic Pages 88

The Autobiography of Benjamin Franklin *by Benjamin Franklin*   ISBN: *1-59462-135-7*   **$24.95**
The Autobiography of Benjamin Franklin has probably been more extensively read than any other American historical work, and no other book of its kind has had such ups and downs of fortune. Franklin lived for many years in England, where he was agent... Biographies/History Pages 332

Name	
Email	
Telephone	
Address	
City, State ZIP	

☐ **Credit Card**   ☐ **Check / Money Order**

Credit Card Number	
Expiration Date	
Signature	

Please Mail to: Book Jungle
PO Box 2226
Champaign, IL 61825
or Fax to: 630-214-0564

ORDERING INFORMATION
web*: www.bookjungle.com*
email*: sales@bookjungle.com*
fax*: 630-214-0564*
mail*: Book Jungle PO Box 2226 Champaign, IL 61825*
or PayPal *to sales@bookjungle.com*

Please contact us for bulk discounts

DIRECT-ORDER TERMS

**20% Discount if You Order
Two or More Books**
Free Domestic Shipping!
Accepted: Master Card, Visa,
Discover, American Express